I0594352

the
spiritual
flu

JUSTIN STEWART

Supported and inspired by my beautiful wife
whom I love beyond words
You are the woman to whom
I dedicate my each and every breath
And the soul with which I share
the eternal flame of forever.

*'A loving life of kindly deeds
A helping hand to those in need
Sincere and true in heart and mind
What beautiful memories to leave behind.'*

*Dedicated to you, I took you back into my heart,
and forever walk with you hand in hand
through eternity, with you as my guiding light.*

The mind thinks.
The heart knows.

INTRODUCTION

THE CONTAGION
OF CONSCIOUSNESS

The Spiritual Flu is the contagion of consciousness. It is a multi-dimensional plague, a virus that incubates and envelops our experience of life, in veiled illusion. It is the virus of separation, an embedded spiritual infection functioning to severely suppress our consciousness.

It serves to compromise the possibility of attaining spiritual actualisation; the fulfillment of the promise naturally inherent in our consciousness vehicle. It subversively masks access to one's true spiritual nature, seeking to diminish the potential for us to seat our own powerful inner light and emanate in full expression.

It is a covert condition that has genetically infiltrated the multi-dimensionality of the human being, enforcing its intrusive signature upon the mind, the body and the spirit.

It harnesses and capitalises on the repressive nature of the personality matrix and its carnivorous negative ego, progressively attaining dominance. It manifests a level of psycho-spiritual disharmony, where the higher heart intelligence, is overrun by the unbridled lower egoic personality, rendering two fractured aspects of an intended whole conflicted, rather than in coherent alignment. It is an artificial order of dissonance, where one's potential expansion of consciousness is grossly hindered.

It seeks to impose a terminal disconnect by suppressing any congruence with the higher self. It progressively burdens the soul with an unrelenting and immensely discordant energetic load. It envelops us externally, and it incubates internally, inevitably expressing itself through observable manifest symptoms in the physical body.

It nourishes itself through an anchored confinement within the illusion that all that exists is only that which is perceivable through the five senses. This enslavement to the fire walled boundaries of the material net, leads to the continual depletion of the soul's expression. Under this casted shadow of darkness, compounded by factors of environment, society, teachings and programming, it is able to continue its passage, flourishing into an all encompassing plague.

The planet and its people, have suffered *The Spiritual Flu* for many centuries, many thousands upon millions of years. It is a spiritual level of disease that has permeated our collective consciousness with its digressive influence. It has become so fundamentally ingrained, that it has produced repetitive cycles of human incarnates inheriting this virus of separation.

Many languish in the hypnotic stagnation of this inflicted spiritual condition, falling into the reversal currents of descension. It brings with it an implanted inorganic perception that we as human beings, are separate from source, separate from one another, from the very earth we walk upon and separate from the solar system, galaxy and universe that hosts our human experience. It is a superimposed, inverted, false and spiritually damaging perception of reality to hold, for such an immaculately conceived work of perfection.

As the sands of history funnel through time, we have as a collective, been severed of our connection, and therefore, our innate means to navigate this cosmos. We have suffered from the amnesia, forgotten our truth, our power and our purpose. We have been consequently guided towards a shift away from sovereignty and full consciousness expression. For humankind has, throughout history, been concentrated squarely on the nature of *things*, and the acquisition of those things solely residing in the material realm. Thus, in contravention to its natural inclination, humanity has become fractured and confused, primarily concerned with the physical, rather than the spiritual.

The Spiritual Flu takes its origins in deeply malignant roots. As a consequence of this deep ancestral trauma, our quest to overcome *The Flu* has become a fundamental and necessary part of our process in healing, learning and maturation. It is critical in the reclamation of our species, and therefore, an integral catalyst for affecting change. It is the mechanism through which we shift the future evolution of our consciousness back onto an upward trajectory.

It is a universally prevalent condition for which the remedy lies in reconciling the separation from source. The quest for personal healing therefore, requires we navigate ourselves through a personal journey intended on transcending the dualistic schism of polarity.

In order to become truly empowered, one must identify where the sickness and the infection actually exists. For if one cannot see the infection, and refuses to recognise the darkness that seeks to destroy the light, then it cannot be inoculated. This is the path to healing both the personal consciousness, and that of the human race.

Whilst the remedy to this contagion commands that each of us commit to an ongoing journey of healing and growth, the antidote to this condition, once transmuted and in remission, resides in the revelation of pure simplicity. The key is in the quiet union and attunement to the now moment; this is where one naturally aligns with the flowing waves of the universe.

Turning inward and back into ourselves, reignites the flame of our eternal connection, and returns us to the still point of source, where we are able to perceive the oneness; where we are one, and one is all. Herein describes the true zero-point, the point of singularity, where no separation or division exists between us as the reflections of source, and source itself. For we are in truth, in the essence of our divinity, as one with our creator. We are all the children of Mother Earth, created in the reflection of God. It is only through the beauty of diversity that we differ; in so much that, we are all individuated expressions of that one eternal source of creation.

We are born of this eternal spiritual energy, setting sail on course an apparently linear timeline; handicapped drivers at the helm of a mortal vessel of technological perfection, the human biological organism. But never at any time, do we cease to exist as infinite spiritual beings. We are never limited to that of a finite physical body, nor ever fundamentally defined by one single experience of life, by name, status or reputation. We are an eternal being, a spirit; we are electric and we are magnetic, our physical vehicle a miraculous holographic projection of light and sound. What we are is infinite consciousness observing the three-dimensional physical world of matter, where time is experienced in space.

At this time humanity is undergoing a metamorphosis. We observe the imminent dawning of a new collective consciousness, when the global community peers into the great abyss, with an enhanced clarity and a burgeoning awareness. These are the days of the collective retraction inward. We all retract into the isolation of spiritual self-inquiry, in order to then participate in the reckoning of our rebirth, each of us moving forward in the projection of our soul's most divine expression. As we each work through this individual process of incension, re-establishing the innerconnection, we in turn reconnect the whole and the immediate universal realm as one. We waken, alleviated of the amnesia, remembering more of our lost history and begin to walk back into the light of truth. We ascend into the gnosis of our own individual truth, and the truth of our macrocosmic existence. We re-establish our connection with each other, as an interconnected humanity; brothers and sisters unified by love.

As we focus our attention within, and reclaim the heart consciousness of love, compassion and kindness, we reconcile the inner separation, and the outer separation; the within, and the without. Each small and seemingly insignificant step forward, that an individual takes into the heart space, subsequently propels us all forward into the realisation of a brighter future. When we shift our own frequency, our own perception and therefore, our experience of reality, we then consequentially become collectively encompassed by an uplifting, amplified light force. We come to recognise that this is an evolutionary leap that we are destined to take together, as each individual has both the capacity and the power to contribute significant change in the world.

As we slowly move toward critical mass, we as a people function to elevate the planet's frequency. We transcend the earthly restrictions of the past that imposed false illusions of self, and the ideology that material reality is wholly representative of the human experience. We begin to sense the inspirational energies around us; we begin to observe reality in all its wonderful synchronicity and admire the beauty that surrounds us, irrespective of how bleak the outerscape appears. It is the gestation leading to an imminent rebirth, where we perceive of a new version of ourselves, reborn, not into a new time, but into a new space in time.

We stand at the completion stage in a long cycle and the culmination of a forgettable timeline in our history, the structures of the old world undergo a death and a decay, and so too do we; as all is all, all reflects all. We suffer a metaphorical death, our old toxic ways of being, decay into the past, forging the new road ahead. Through the collective dark night of the soul, we face a tumultuous period of change, where we return to the integrated unity of truth, aligned with the source of our genesis.

With the dawn of the Fifth World drawing near, tremendously powerful and benevolent forces of light and sound permeate our realm, providing a long-awaited window of opportunity. Our Earth sequentially seeds these incoming higher harmonic waves of plasmic energy emanating from the galactic core. We simultaneously undergo bio-regenesis through the reactivation of latent DNA, which increases our light quotient and prepares the physical body for greater health, harmony and the exponentially higher base level of awareness.

We gradually accrete energy building to a level of consciousness which supersedes the density of the third dimension. It seats us in the fourth dimensional intelligence of the heart, expanding out into fifth dimensional consciousness. Love and unity become the dominant archetypes on the planet once again, and our once repressed, inherent higher sensory abilities come online. This evolutionary transit unlocks the gates, opening the passage leading to enlightenment; the full embodiment of the human being's bio-spiritual potential.

During the ascension phase, Mother Earth fertilises a clear passage through which we ascend as one collective; a unified body of consciousness residing harmoniously with, and upon her miraculous living body that is our home. This is a shared journey of cosmic evolutionary experience.

Through the realisation of each person's higher purpose and fulfillment of soul mission, we ultimately move upward together, into a new age of peace and harmony. This is the great awakening, when the human family wakes from the eons of deep sleep, heals, recalibrates and restores its intended organic divine blueprint. It is to be a newly transformed experience of life, projected from rejuvenated architecture, animating a more congruent perception of reality.

We return to an ascending state of consciousness, bathed in the solar light and higher frequencies of being; the frequencies of revelation, reclamation, liberation and emancipation, hallmarking a successful planetary and biological ascension. It signifies the return to singularity, where the inner masculine principle merges in sacred marriage with the inner feminine principle, and the child is born, resurrecting the holy trinity.

We become cosmically sovereign citizens peacefully forging a harmonious world, sharing one heart and projecting one vision, the vision of love as all we need to flourish.

SYNOPSIS

This is a story of awakening into a higher state of conscious awareness, and an account of the personal learnings, discoveries and experiences encountered on the exploratory journey through ascension, on the path toward enlightenment. It is through the insightful narrative of one individual's heroic navigation toward hierogamic union, that we ourselves may take inspiration, and continue courageously onward in our own personal journey of remembrance, reintegrating our own heroic light.

The Spiritual Flu, as expressed in Noah's story, is characterised by the commonplace trauma of separation, the resultant sense of isolation and the fear of abandonment and betrayal; compounded by a negatively programmed subconscious mind, a dominant negative ego self construct, fear of the future and a distinctly frustrating lack of true divine spiritual purpose.

As we experience life projected through the mortal lens of Noah, we traverse the antithesis of challenging lows and breathtaking highs. We experience the euphoria of the surrender, the release accompanying ego death, and the gestational period when new life is manifesting within, birthing him back into spiritual coherence. It is this ultimate state of realisation, of reckoning, of reconciliation, becoming and contentment, that we all inevitably seek beneath each breath we take.

It is through this relatable story of courage, persistence, dedication and discernment, that we may truly innerstand, that the promise of self-actualisation is attainable by all people on this planet.

the

spiritual

flu

JUSTIN STEWART

I

THE RIGHT OF PASSAGE

Ancient Nordic wisdom once decreed that in order to experience positive growth and change in the cycle of self-transformation, one was required to walk through the passage of darkness. For this is a fundamental element in the cycle of perpetual renewal. As in nature, the progression of this cycle entails, a death, a decay, a fertilisation, a gestation and a rebirth.

Noah's body of mortal flesh carried something precious, a soul, and an old one at that. He had been born into this world armed with many talents and attributes, accompanied by the energetic sensitivities inherent in members of the highly coded Indigo children. He possessed a great capacity to think analytically, broadly and philosophically, and had been successful in achieving great things in his life. In addition to a wise disposition and sharp intellect, he was physically polished, a natural athlete. He took pride in his appearance, and was confident in his own skin. He was however, uncomfortable with being purely judged on his looks, as if that was all he had to offer the world. He wanted people to know him for his deep and authentic self, rather than a polished outer shell to be objectified.

Spirituality and the exploration of the theosophical always took on a prominent focus in his days. He was an intuitive being and recollected past lives. He would elaborately recount these prior material world experiences, to those interested, eloquently detailing times as a Tibetan monk, an indigenous medicine woman, a poet, and as a grail-keeper of the Christ Templar.

Noah though, in this lifetime, had grown to forty-three years of age. He embodied the strength of the masculine balanced with feminine sensibility and vulnerability. He was relatively quiet, shy some would say, but possessed a free-spirit. An enthusiastic traveller and inquisitor of this world, and of others, he was a modern day explorer. He was by birthright a philosopher, and had undertaken the study of such, both Greek and ancient, whilst at university. He maintained this studious curiosity, delving further into ancient texts and teachings. He admired the great scholars who often risked their own mortality, daring to peek into the unknown, into potentiality and the realm of infinite awareness — into the nature of source and creation itself.

Adopting various spiritual practices of choice along his journey, he regularly called on the support of angels and guides, despite the fact he couldn't *see* them. He wasn't overly clairvoyant, well as an adult anyway. He delved deeply into alternative modalities, theories on history and the nature of the reality we exist in. He was fascinated by the possibility of worlds that existed in different dimensions, the worlds existing simultaneously alongside this world, the ones in the higher realms, in the quantum space of the infinite. His passionate efforts had focused upon the process of relentless questioning — the questioning of everything within this life here as we know it. He sought to query, interpret, deconstruct and understand the physical world, the universe, the cosmos and beyond, gaining more insight from his aptitude for introspection, than from anything material that the external world had to offer. His feeling, his knowing on a deeper internal level, was that there was an aspect of him which held the answers to the mysteries, to the story of his higher self. This was the elusive part of him that didn't comprehend stress, wasn't fearful of life's trials and hadn't resolved to a bleaker future of melancholic repetition.

Over the past decade the basic means of existence were sustained through working as a health coach. Prior to this vocation, he had departed a career in advertising spanning some twelve years. For with integrity as his predominant virtue, he had grown tired and found increasing difficulty in selling superfluous things he didn't believe in, despite the high salaries. He was operating outside the moral and ethical boundaries of what felt authentic to his true nature. Eventually, this frustration rendered the six-figure pay cheques meaningless, and ignited significant motivation to fearlessly re-direct his focus toward the attainment of true fulfillment. As such, he had been intuitively led to pursue the area of physical health and wellbeing for work — a completely different vocational path, and this represented an almighty leap of faith. He envisaged this new direction more in tune with his essence; one that would provide the platform upon which to express himself with more authenticity and offer real value to people.

Nonetheless, the predominant feeling he digested commonly, was the sense of his personal potential being unrequited. He knew very well that he wasn't living his *'true purpose'* nor had fulfilled his potential, and this pained him greatly. Irrespective of the vocation of the time, the uniform or the title adorning the business card, it was the altruistic perspective on life that was, for him, constant and effervescent. It bubbled away at the very depths of his true nature. He was highly imaginative and this didn't always lend itself well within the thinking mind of a person unfulfilled.

As time passed, he grew increasingly cynical with the modern world. How it had been selfishly and negligently constructed for the profit of the few, and of how the majority of people simply mirrored these attributes, behaving with the same selfishness and greed. It was a perplexing reality upon which to observe. People were separated, desensitised and vampiric, devoid of love, treating each other poorly, with judgement, with racism and bigotry. This made for a toxic and depressive perception and experience of life on the outside. He resigned to the fact, that human beings were a damaged species and one that had, as a consequence, not only inflicted *self*-harm, but also more broadly, had inflicted harm on our Mother, the Earth. This bore a sense of hopelessness in changing anything. This physical world was one he eventually summated as dark, leaving him feeling despondent, isolated and lost.

Largely, this matrix of chaos he had landed in, when he was birthed into this world, was the expression of a humankind that had lost its way, progressively falling further from their connection to organic source. This distorted reality had been orchestrated through an inversion of natural law superimposed upon us all, where controlling forces manage an artificial system of enslavement. A consumptive model where we the people, as energetic commodities, residing behind the veil of limited awareness, are kept in the dark. All the while, these self-professed illuminated overlords hoard the sacred knowledge of the intelligence fields and manipulate the mechanics of creation, effectively, locking the corridors to truth. Consequently, it has been made near impossible for the human race to access their rightful spiritual sovereignty and full embodiment — for so long as man remained disempowered, *they* remained empowered, capitalising from the systematic abuse and subjugation of the collective. Through hybridised bloodlines, shadow governments, secret groups and orders, this virulent off-planet, human and non-human, exo-political agenda had subversively branched out into a surface network. The invaders had, for millennia, manipulated and suppressed our perception of reality. They stole and guarded the great secrets of history and the nature of our universe, erasing the memory of our true cosmogenesis. Over time this has represented concerted and organised efforts to diminish the human expression into that of a dream spell, keeping us hypnotised, unaware and unconscious to the truth; for laying dormant within the infinite potential of the human being, is the capacity for such things as telepathy, inter-dimensional travel and the alchemy of matter. Thus, of the highest priority, has been the ongoing suppression of this truth, at all costs, from public knowledge — for if the common man was to know of the truth, he would know of his power.

Unearthing this nefarious historical conspiracy had been a hard cross for Noah to bear. Mankind, it seemed, had been chartered off course, towards probable large scale disaster and irreversible peril, unless a major shift occurred. Noah, despite having built a solid understanding and comprehension of these interconnected truths, managed to sustain an innate belief in the potential of humankind to reconcile its mistakes and liberate itself back onto the path of love. Fuelling this vision, was his faith in something greater, of a higher purpose, for humankind, and for his experience of life. He maintained the hope that the forces of light, of good, would eventually prevail over evil, over the darkness that had cast a shadow over the world.

Accompanying him every single step of the journey for the last eight years had been his twin flame and wife, Aurora. Noah loved her deeply and emphatically the moment he saw her. Albeit, this unexpected epiphany had transpired at a stage in his life, when falling in love with her set up the most challenging of circumstances. Circumstances that entailed the charting of a monumentally new course in his personal journey, in the name of love.

Aurora was tall, brandished striking dark features and had a strong energetic presence. A natural beauty, she was goddess-like and of Mediterranean descent. She wore beautiful long hair, had broad shoulders, long shapely legs and earthy eyes like that of a lion. She oozed personality and vibrance — rather more outgoing than her partner, making for an ideal balance. Despite being eleven years his junior, she was emotionally mature and wise beyond her years. She possessed an inner strength, which had been solidified through her endurance of childhood, confronting immense upheaval, abuse and instability.

Aurora left an indelible mark on anyone she met, such was her likeable and magnetic persona. She was larger than life. She abounded in positivity and joie de vivre. Noah marvelled at how she beamed with light and radiated joyous energy. She was fun, fun and more fun! With her Sun in Leo, a true lioness and an enthusiastic student of astrology, her gift was her resonance with children. Children loved her and gravitated strongly to her abundant love, empathetic nature and playful energy. She had committed much of her teens and early adulthood to developing opportunities for children (a contribution to her community that was unparalleled). The potential reality of becoming a mother, and the mother of Noah's child, had brewed in her the deepest of dreams.

He respected her greatly, particularly given what she had endured in the past. It had been enough to have snuffed out the brightest of flames. In addition to being the black sheep of the family she existed as an outsider in the world, she was sensitive, deep, powerful and a high vibrational elder amongst souls. Aurora's spirit, much the same as Noah's, also yearned for discovery, for magic and the spiritual truth. The same bugbears and questions burning within Noah, burned furiously away in her mind too, all the things we all reflect upon over the years of our lives — the nature of our purpose, the pursuit of inner peace and enlightenment, the powers of healing and how to transcend the matrix we find ourselves in. She too, aspired to live as her soul's best expression. This meant freedom from the baggage of the past and the space to become truly magical, manifesting anything she wanted in the future.

Generation after generation human beings have searched for the answers, the answers to the same questions. Where do we come from? What are we doing here? What is the meaning of life? What is my purpose?

Why do we feel so disconnected? Where do we go when we pass on?

Both wanted to journey the breadth of the truth, and to live as their unlimited potential. They had made a commitment to themselves, and to each other, that they would approach life with a dedication to expansion, in order to reach the conclusions to these great questions.

As time passed during the early years of their relationship and post-wedding, their love flourished, yet they felt smothered and suppressed by their routine.

In order to discover anything new, be it a physical world discovery or a profound spiritual realisation, it requires that we apply a different perspective; to observe ourselves and our world differently. Einstein speaks of insanity, as doing the same thing over and over again, and expecting different results. Spiritual growth, therefore, lay not in the practice of mindless automated repetition, but in the practice of courageous exploration — to see things differently, do things differently and make decisions you would otherwise resist making. It is to evolve through the process of change; and change invariably requires overcoming the natural human tendency to fear the unknown. It commands one apply the courage of their convictions and bravely dive into uncharted waters.

Intuiting stagnation, they soon realised they were not truly living a life enriched with meaning. Any dreams smouldered away as unfulfilled potential, in danger of being lost to the sands of time. Their innate ability to generate dynamic change of their own volition had been temporarily forgotten, and the prevalent state of being was one of physical, mental and emotional tiredness. The contagion was incubating through their mind, body and their spirit. Each morning Noah would sit at the side of the bed and utter the same line.

'I can't do this anymore, I feel like I'm dying.'

Both had suffered severe emotional trauma, to put it mildly, confronting much in the dawning days of their relationship, including the despairing separation from Noah's son James, imposed through the cessation of visitation rights. Recent times had also burdened the pair having encountered the torridly scarring experience of Aurora's first cousin's suicide and the death of a young man, the brother to a close friend of Aurora, who passed on after succumbing to a single unprovoked blow to the head.

Their now larger than necessary house, the locale and the entire environment only served as an agonising reminder of those happenings, and of their broader past. It had become an undeniable necessity for the couple to relocate somewhere new. Despite having established a wonderful home and an exciting business venture, they grew loathsome of the burdensome weight of the past, the dense energy of their home city, its unpleasantly cold climate and the preposterously high cost of living.

Noah encountered immense difficulty in dealing with the over-bearing pain of the unjust detachment from his child. There was a routine refusal to go upstairs, into James' part of the house, as that only delivered a cascade of memories that were all too painful to contend with.

For Noah, this confronting reality had driven home what appeared a final and unforgiving blow of permanence. It lodged itself into the damaged aspect of him, which held the pain and trauma stemming from the death of his beloved maternal grandmother, and then his doting stepfather the following year. These were loved ones to whom he depended on for stability, guidance and for nurturing; the metaphorical roots of his life had been starved of nutrients at the brittle age of twenty-one. Maimed by grief and sadness, he had never since been able to process and release the pain. He floundered in a sense of loss and clung to fading memories of when they'd been alive. He had never found the clarity, the strength nor the want to let them go. This collective pain and trauma rooted deeply in his emotional body; it was a calamity of detrimental proportions.

When you travel with the luggage of the past, that pain and sadness cultivates fear; fear of an uncertain future, fear of what else may go wrong, who else may pass away and what else we may lose. It's the point at which one can begin living in the past, inadvertently creating a distasteful future. The moment, the now, never comes into existence, never sees the light of day, it's a cycle of fear and negative projection which forms the personal reality of experience, further compounded by the inorganic, densely geared structures of society.

This leads one into a state of victimhood, whereby the victim interprets themselves as being at the mercy of forces not in their control. It is a mentality whereby one merely hopes to not fall *victim* to fate. It is an attitude where our own experience and very mortality is assumed to be under the complete control of external forces, that we believe we fall victim to, and have no power over. Living life immersed in the victim psychology, from the 'I have no control' mentality, is perhaps one of the greatest traps we fall into, and this has been a trap further perpetuated by many doctrines of belief. Most encapsulate their experience from the sense, that the mission is to *survive* this experience, not truly *experience* it, through actively creating it. The unfortunate goal becomes the mission of merely attempting to survive life, to see out a procession of years relatively unscathed, which culminates in old age then death. Commonly, when people do make it there, the conclusion is often drawn that the individual had a *lucky* life, as though fate had decided to be merciful on them, and not another.

The truth in life is that there is only the learning through manifest experience to serve our higher purpose and soul growth. Pain, trauma and suffering is not the higher objective of the experience, it is only ever a byproduct of it, and does not equate in the realms in which your highest self exists. All experience is interconnected, carries reason and ultimate purpose for each soul. It is through the forging of virtue, of trust, courage, inner-guidance and self-sovereignty, that we cultivate the ability to create our future. We have the power to direct the screenplay, rather than render ourselves down, as the diminished actors in an externally dictated play.

II

UPON THE WINDS OF CHANGE

Noah and Aurora had experienced the gamut of human emotions since meeting. These experiences weighted heavily — the world around had become too familiar, stale and empty. The winds of change grew in vitality blowing stronger and stronger.

At times in life we all need change, of a different shape or size, sometimes it's a subtle change, sometimes extreme. Change is always developing, coming, always manifesting and taking shape. Change as we know, is central to the system of the universe, a universal law if you will. As all energy moves in the perpetual cycles of change, then by virtue, so do we. We either resist change, or embrace it towards our own betterment. We are in a state of constant change — each moment denotes change, change from the moment before. It is to be accepted, as it is inherent and fundamental to life. Change should not be fought nor feared. It must be embraced as otherwise it tends to move faster, drive harder and challenge us more. That's when the 'wake-up calls' come — when we can't see, or *refuse* to see the procession of signs.

When it's your time for change, your *divine* time, you will know of it. On some level, within some aspect of yourself, you'll find yourself peering into the eye of the storm, swept up into the vortex and flung out into a new direction. When these storms pass through our lives our inclination can be to run, hide, hibernate and sit it out till it passes. We have the natural tendency to self-preserve in efforts to remain safe, and ultimately survive. In these moments, taking any action perceived as risk, can activate fear, and fear is both debilitating and counter-productive. But in the brave making of decisions, in the taking of risks and the facing of one's fears, we discover an innate capacity, and grow the wings with which to fly — this is when liberation occurs. For an instant the tumultuous energies spiral you out of fear and confusion into the light where the possibilities open up and what seemed unthinkable before, rapidly manifests into potential for existence.

The couple decided to take the leap and travel abroad. They closed the business they had worked so tirelessly to build, packed up the household and sold everything material in their lives that didn't serve them any longer. They lightened their load, relinquishing any attachment and obligation to the old. No longer would they be reminded of the past everywhere they went, the future was to be completely new, well externally anyway.

The day of the flight departing the country that had accommodated their past, arrived. In the lead up, they had been subjected to an onslaught of perplexed looks, endless questioning and projections of negativity. This is all a common experience for those seeking to explore, striving to exit the matrix of normality and forge ahead in the name of spiritual growth. The system and its living components only seek to maintain the status quo, which is to keep those who attempt to escape, imprisoned. Nonetheless, they had made the definitive decision that they were in fact, releasing themselves from the ties that bind.

On a wing and a prayer, the plane increased its speed down the runway and took off with the two lovers on board destined for the unknown. As the winds took hold of the aircraft, Noah peered out the window, reciting a great and favourite poem that he took particular inspiration from. It spoke to him, it expressed the power of taking control and then living as the master of one's life, in total freedom.

'Invictus'

Out of the night that covers me,
Black as the pit from pole to pole,
I thank whatever gods may be
For my unconquerable soul.

In the fell clutch of circumstance
I have not winced nor cried aloud.
Under the bludgeonings of chance
My head is bloody, but unbowed.

Beyond this place of wrath and tears
Looms but the horror of the shade,
And yet the menace of the years
Finds and shall find me unafraid.

It matters not how strait the gate,
How charged with punishments the scroll,
I am the master of my fate,
I am the captain of my soul.

— *William Ernest Henley*

Once that flight had taken off, life on the outside had become a blank canvas once again. When we are called upon to trust in our own ability to make decisions from balanced neutrality and pure intention, it requires of us that we retract, look deep inside and embrace our spirit which is courageous. It is at these moments we integrate with source, we feel the creator and the true intrinsic nature of it all from within our own inner world. The truth is always accessible within this space. Upon reflection of these times, looking back in retrospect, is when you will appreciate the magic. It will be confirmation as to how the pieces fit, how the puzzle comes together and you will feel whole, a sense of oneness. From disengaged to present, from separate to together, from darkness to love. This growing awareness and acknowledgement rebuilds the disconnect with our higher self and both energies begin to harmoniously synthesise — the material self with the spiritual self.

For four years they ventured far and wide travelling, exploring, discovering, questioning and working. Through Asia, Europe and back through South-East Asia, six countries, different provinces, aromas, scenes, faces, places, people, curiosities and tragedies.

Ultimately, they chose one of the hotter, more humid, tropical places to call their base. This new place qualified on all fronts as the ideal environment with which to restore, renew, rebuild and flourish. It was a quieter place, with fantastic weather and a generally simpler, slower lifestyle. People still walked the streets at dawn, greeted strangers with respect and openness, they had friendships that were nurtured. They sold fruits and vegetables of their own labour from tiny motorised stalls, monks trod the pavements barefoot each morning and butterflies the size of birds, freely flew amongst feathered beings, large and small all in harmony. It was an unspoilt environment, it was symbolic of places on Earth from times now long ago, before the wave of material advancement came, before corporations and before deforestation occurred without thought, in the name of progress, 'human' progress. This was a place where that progress had not yet fully grasped the land and sinfully spewed its calamity over the hot, humid densely treed tropical paradise. Perhaps Buddha himself had bestowed the wisdom of gratitude here, gratitude for the diversity and beauty of our planet, at least of this small expression of it set just above the equatorial line.

They had both chosen to simplify life, live less materially and more spiritually in order to bridge the gap, reconnect and find the peace within. Noah had never felt so loved, and so in love in his entire life. He had through his union with Aurora gained back that nurturing stability. That consistent love aspect that is invaluable in setting the scene for the process to begin, for the gates that lead to the path of transcendence to open. On a deeply personal emotional level, he had reached a point, prior to taking the plunge and selling up the old, where he sensed that it was time to turn his awareness inward, face the inner conflict, reconcile his traumas and begin to foster his designed potential.

What was it that had been holding him back?

Who did he want to be in this world?

Life now necessitated he locate the solutions to these cryptic psycho-spiritual problems. For he knew that he wasn't expressing the optimum version of himself, and besides, he owed his love that gift, in return for the true love she had brought into his life. She deserved that.

He would continuously assess his life in the same ways we all do — we overthink, over-rationalise, unfairly judge and ridicule, ourselves! We all fall towards behaviours that are self-destructive. We self-sabotage and become more and more disconnected, governed by an automatic (unconscious) entity, which can unfortunately become the most dominant aspect; one that is repressive to the purest, most loving expression of ourselves. We then carry this fragmented aspect of us, a manufactured personality that 'gets in the way' of maximising our potential, stifling the fulfillment of dreams. It creates a perception block in terms of re-integrating with the unseen part of us; that part that can be brought into the physical, serving to balance us. What we grow to perceive and create for ourselves is an illusion, projected through the negative ego construct; a warped lens of perception, manifesting a separateness within, and without. We separate ourselves from mother nature, our brothers and sisters, the organic wave forms of the universe, and everything that is love.

Noah had become increasingly aware of, and fully acknowledged, that the sense of isolation, the fear, trauma, pain, and the unnerving frustration that something was missing, was symptomatic of a set of deeply ingrained multi-dimensional issues. These were internal schisms that had absolutely nothing to do with any material world shortcomings or scarcities. The desperation in the knowing that he hadn't exorcised the ghosts of his past and integrated his divinity, was the one thing that was missing in his life and the one thing he needed to accomplish in order to reach personal fulfillment, and be at peace. He longed for that time, for the feeling it would bring, but often considered it implausible, impossible and unlikely, for spiritual progress is immensely difficult to measure. These things can't be seen, they can only be felt. Whilst growth was progressively being achieved, it all too often seemed not to be the case. Noah, unbeknownst to him, had encountered his major karmic tests; he'd been tried, tested and tortured many times. Even since knowing Aurora he had experienced many lifetimes worth of heartbreaking trials, tribulations and learnings. He had grown tired of the prevailing helplessness attached to the objective of healing, remembering and discovering his purpose. His time hadn't come to have his burdens alleviated. There had been no magic pill, no angel had swooped in, taken his pain and flown it away into the void. He resigned to the fact that the only way out of a hole too deep to leap out of, would be to climb his way out.

Noah had mind-crafted a metaphorical hell over the decades of his life, which had taken a front seat in the space located right between his ears. It was the kind of desperate place on the precipice of eternal damnation, the absolute expression of blackness and where gluttonous emptiness found sustenance. His frustrations had reached tipping point, the death before the decay had reached its critical mass, had infested long enough, deeply enough and it was a brewing insurgent. It was the darkness before the dawn — it was the onset of the *Spiritual Flu's* capacity to lead one through the dark night of the soul. He had reached the stage in his life where he was ready to be propelled into that very personal place we all have within, to come face to face with his reality, his pain and his emptiness, only he hadn't the inclination that the time had come.

III

THE OVUM AMIDST THE DECAY

In the tropics during the monsoons the onset of the wind invariably signals rain, and a lot of it. The heavy deluges, the storms that pass destroy, but also at the same time revitalise the lands they touch. This is the sensitively balanced ecosystem of life.

The couple had settled in well to their idyllic new residence, delighting in the consistently bright, sunny days and quiet clear water beaches upon which to enjoy early morning walks. Given their combined experience and unique skill set, they swiftly secured an ideal management position at a state-of-the-art health club nearby, and this stability rapidly reinvigorated a great dream they both shared — to bring a child of their own into the world.

The likelihood of that potential materialising posed a set of profound challenges in its own right, given the decisions made by Noah in the past — prior to meeting with the eternal eyes of Aurora, Noah had electively chosen to surgically sever his testicular passages permanently, by virtue of vasectomy. He had seen to it that his seed would no longer be able to bear fruit, in what at the time, and under the prevailing circumstance, appeared an appropriate course of action. However, once he had the realisation that the relationship with Aurora was one of divine union, a regretful black cloud formed over Noah's life, raining down a tremendous deluge of anxiety over the future implications.

Aurora, clearly aware of the predicament this represented for both of them, and ever the optimist, honourably chose not to allow it to perturb her, nor prevent her from wholeheartedly pursuing the real love she felt between them, despite the ramifications of what Noah had done. Both knew that in the future, there were various alternate avenues with which they could pursue, deciding to place such matters on hold, until the time came to explore the available options.

Noah admonished himself for this decision. He wished that he could have teleported back into that time and not decide on that course of action. That painful process of severance a decade and a half prior had worked all too well, for he in medical terms was advised that he could not give Aurora what they both so longed for, a child — *their* child.

Prior to departing for their travels, they had seen to the consequential and immensely costly procedure of rectifying this block of the path leading from him to her. The highly regarded surgeon back in their home town had made his best efforts to re-join the tubules (perform a reversal) and pave the way once again for his patient's DNA information to be expressed through the regular means of conception. The doctor was supremely confident in what he was able to achieve, assuring the couple of a cleanly performed reconnection, suggestive of an uninterrupted flow. However, after some time had elapsed following the reversal procedure, there had been no pregnancy. Neither the change to a healthier environment, nor the liberated lifestyle in the freedom outside of the matrix, had seemingly made any difference. Many days of morning meditation, stress-free living, fresh organic food, memorable experiences and joyous moments passed, yet hadn't provided what both had expected. Not withstanding that life now presented a plethora of positive distractions and endless possibilities, both sensed that there was action to be taken. There was to be no more ignoring the elephant in the room, as it had become obvious that something was wrong.

As such, the couple were compelled to make a visit to a urology specialist in the city to get the facts. Two long hours expired in nervous wait for the results and through they came, zero — no trace of his seed had been found. The report detailed a zero sperm count, *azoospermia,* as they call it. The dysfunctional state of Noah's reproductive system had been confirmed via the stark insensitivity of the medical industry in plain black and white. He was for all intent and purposes branded sterile via the clinical diagnosis, although in probability, Noah simply presented with a condition symptomatic of scar tissue.

To wear the label of *sterility*, was a burdensome weight to bear for the man, particularly when he so longed to share the love with his partner through the expression of a child. It brought on a sense of total and utter emasculation. It sunk Noah's heart. He found difficulty in corresponding what he had just seen to his wife, who was intently awaiting a positive outcome, one which he could not offer.

It was a confronting potential reality for both of them in their own individual ways. For Noah, who had experienced the joys of fatherhood before, he drowned in emotional despair, entertaining thoughts of 'what if she'll leave me if I can't give her a child.' For Aurora it was a difficult proposition to remain supportive and not act beaten, for the viability of her physical functions were not in question. This was a heartbreaking truth for both Noah, and for Aurora to process. Was their love to be left unrequited in relation to children? If there were to be one thing true love was deserving of, it was that it be enabled to be exulted through co-creation.

With some hope of a miracle (as they can be manifested), Noah had nightly attempted to energetically heal his issue to no avail. He imagined light around the disconnect, dissolving the blockage through mind projection, thereby psychically reinstating the fluid passage for the objective of manifesting new physical life — the divine flower of their union.

Once the time had come to investigate the remaining options available to them, beyond an immaculate conception, they were buoyed to discover that modern medicine offered couples, finding themselves in a like predicament, with an avenue to parenthood, albeit at great expense. It was with mixed feelings to discover that all hope was not lost; the final option available to them would entail interfacing with the vexatious pharmaceutical industry. A transnational leviathan, founded in false science, corruption and gross negligence, paired with an untrustworthy allopathic medical system, one premised on sickness, rather than health, profit over prevention and the proliferation of the artificial over the organic. It brought forth a serious moral dilemma, one which they encountered tremendous difficulty in reconciling, irrespective of their desire to become mother and father.

This last bastion entailed surgery and the exploration of Noah's testicles in order to retrieve the material that was required for the process of artificial fertilisation to begin. For they were certain that despite the long ago severance, despite the apparent failure of the attempt to reinstate the tubes, and the still vacant void of Aurora's womb, that he was indeed still capable of providing the genetic material necessary for conception to be successful — whether it be through the natural passage of conception, or through western medicine's synthetic and invasive methods.

Three days had passed since Noah celebrated his forty-fourth birthday. An air of strangeness had always accompanied that date, April 11th, that prominent Gregorian marker in time. It was the date that drew the line in the sands of eternity, marking his entrance into this realm. This discordant feeling had forever mystified Noah, the prevailing sense of unease and vulnerability that accompanied every birthday. He figured that it was perhaps a reflection of the difficult birthing he experienced, a vague yet deep-seated memory. Memories of assuming the non-advisable breech posture and the sensation of the large and foreign clasps affixing to his soft under-developed skull. There was also the period in artificial incubation undergoing blue light therapy for seven days following birth, and the scarcity of breastmilk on which to nourish. What adverse impacts had these interventions and immediate separations had then, on the days, years and decades that followed, he would wonder. Did his experience of birth bear any ill effect on the rest of his days? That question burned within awaiting the appropriate answer by way of some sort of profound remembrance.

Noah had welcomed the impending distraction scheduled to fall within the week of his birthday, though the medical procedure set down for the morning had brought much foreboding. The scientific answers that would be gleaned from this short, yet confronting process, would reveal the probability around what they had both envisioned for the future. The exploratory operation was scheduled for 9:30am sharp. No liquid or food was to be taken in the preceding twelve hours beforehand, something that Noah found difficulty in adhering to, given his love for morning espresso. In light of the gravity of what would be investigated by the foreign surgeon, he chose to sleep longer than he would otherwise, calm himself under the shower, dawdle through dressing and make way for the hospital, only minutes away, so as to overcome that visceral want for that bean elixir upon rising.

Accompanied by his wife, they reached the hospital early. The act of arriving early reflected how important a positive outcome was to them. It had to be.

The apprehensive wait for the 'time to go in' verged on agony. The nurses and doctor, unaware of their patient's passionate liking for a good brew, enjoyed their morning refreshment in direct earshot of the man nervously waiting. Noah dismissed thoughts of what it tasted like, choosing instead to close his eyes, breathe out any nerves and wait patiently. The sound of that one last slurp through a straw burst out through the ward.

One of the nurses appeared and motioned for Noah to follow her to the change rooms where he would need to get undressed and adorn a blue operative gown with slippers. Noah removed his t-shirt, shorts and underwear bearing all to no-one but the change room walls. He exited the room and proceeded back to sit down in the waiting area, as directed by the surgeon who had now intimated that the time for the operation was only minutes away. Sheepishly, Noah resumed his position alongside his supportive wife, herself dealing with her own experience of intense emotion and trepidation. Crossing his legs in order to preserve his dignity and not risk the embarrassment of exposing his uncovered genitals, he waited patiently until he was called.

'Okay, it's time to go in now,' the nurse advised.

'The procedure should take thirty-five minutes, all going to plan.'

The couple shared a last warm and tender embrace. Aurora clearly seeing the need for Noah's tension to be relieved even just a little, by the feeling of her loving heart close to his.

'I love you,' Noah confessed.

'I love you too, my sweetheart.'

'Please pray for me, ask our angels, our guides and ask Ninny to be with us during this time more so than ever.'

Ninny, Noah's maternal Grandmother, now twenty-three years deceased, had left an indelible mark on her grandson — such was her natural propensity to love unconditionally and fully. She was a true nurturer. He had mourned her death ever since her sudden passing and carried the grief that her mortal departure was in fact, permanent. He had believed her to be immortal matter and had never entertained the idea that she may die a physical death.

Noah, spreadeagled on the operating table, looked down to see only his feet exposed to the icy air of the theatre, the air conditioning was up higher than it ought to have been. It made the insecurity of the experience that much more uncomfortable as he began to shiver. Three nurses, the surgeon and the anaesthetist had now taken their place, methodically prepping the instruments, the digital screens and the lights, before sending Noah into the sedated void that is full anaesthesia.

'Hi Noah, I'm Ramish, your anaesthetist,' the doctor officiously announced.

Noah offered a short groan in acknowledgement. He then turned his head back to rest, preparing for the needle, he so apprehensively waited for, to be inserted.

'You will feel a slight coldness starting at the tips of your fingers and then moving upwards towards your head,' Ramish explained.

'Once I have administered the sedative you will soon be restful and feel somewhat sleepy.'

Noah lay there for an anxious five minutes whilst the operational crew moved about and did their final checks. He sensed Ramish checking the needle and the intravenous drip that the nurse had inserted into Noah's hand. Perhaps it is true to say that for a human being, one of the most confronting experiences is that of a fully anaesthetised surgery. It calls upon faith, it requires one to relinquish total control of their body and its faculties, presuming an immense trust in those responsible for preserving the safety, life and the wellbeing of the patient.

Noah had entertained all these thoughts in the lead-up to the day that had now come. The need to trust that the anaesthetic be accurately measured and delivered into his helpless body and the need to let go of any fear for his welfare whilst unconscious. The possibility of golden staph, an infected wound, internal bleeding and other complications were all too prevalent possibilities that ought not be affirmed.

'Okay. I will now administer the anaesthetic and we will see you on the other side,' Ramish stated once again in advice.

Noah felt his heart rate elevate awaiting the moment he would encounter the sharp end of the needle insert into his hand, then the onset of the coldness which was predicted to move up his left arm towards his head in quick succession. Through quiet prayer in his mind's eye, he requested his guides, his angels and light worker beings watch over the procedure and ensure that he be returned safely to homeostasis, having gained a positive outcome.

Experiencing a short burst of that predicted cool sensation, he almost instantaneously drifted off. Unapparent to the medical staff, three guides from Noah's personal team of guides and healers seated in a higher dimension, watched meticulously as the surgeon parted Noah's legs to reveal his genital area — this was the area of exploratory focus. Accompanying them were other cosmic family members, Noah's step-father Joseph and his treasured grandmother, Ninny, now a midwife of the spirit caring for those disillusioned with their departures from the Earth (those who had passed their bodies suddenly, or had suicided in the case of Aurora's cousin Shantel).

The busyness and constant utterances in a foreign language alerted a higher aspect of Noah's consciousness as to the progress of the operation. The three guides psychically steered the surgeon to the correct area for which success would be assured — the place where his seed lay resting, his reproductive organs.

Some thirty minutes into the operation the guides had managed to course the tunnels of Noah's manhood, with the surgeon obtaining tissue specimens and extracting seminal fluid, that would be later tested for viability.

Noah was wheeled out of the operating theatre past where Aurora had been sitting busily biting her nails in anxious wait.

'How are you my love?' gently enquiring of her drowsy husband as he was ferried past.

'I'm okay.' Noah muttered looking extremely groggy.

Noah was immediately transferred to the recovery area where a wait of two and a half hours was enforced, in order for the nurses to monitor recovery and ensure he was going to be fit to be returned home. Meanwhile, Aurora enquired with the surgeon as to the success of the procedure.

'Yes, we found what we were looking for, however, it will require further investigation in order to ascertain the viability. Until then we can't be certain of the potential for success.'

This news was almost too profound in its importance for Aurora to digest, so she re-enquired.

'So, you found something? Do you have enough?' Aurora reframing her query, in case something had been lost across the language barrier.

'Yes, but as I stated...'

Aurora immediately contacted Pamela, her mother-in-law, as she had also been eagerly awaiting news of the success, or otherwise, of the operation, and naturally as to the wellbeing of her one and only son.

Aurora gave thought to her beloved in the recovery area. For he had no idea of the success, or otherwise, of the procedure. He was likely still partially intoxicated, dancing with butterflies and riding the imminence of his release, eager to be briefed with the positive answer Aurora had already been privy to.

Noah woke. He immediately convinced himself that he was okay, that he'd made it through the operation and felt grateful to once again witness his surroundings, to smell and move. Where he had been he had no recollection of. Through what space, which realm had he passed through under the influence of the sedation he wondered.

Before too long the desire for a smooth, strong and robust coffee reared its head. Upon noticing a clock up on the wall nearby, he promptly calculated the likely time of departure from recovery.

'How are you feeling Noah?' enquired one of the nurses on duty.

'You may have some water shortly if you like,' to which Noah nodded, planning to imagine it as a piccolo latte sliding down the back of his throat, tantalising his tastebuds.

Two and a half hours passed, much to his dismay. This time had allowed for short power naps and to keep check on the time until he was given the all-clear to be released.

'Okay Noah, I'll take you back now,' another nurse wheeling the chair over beside the stark bed, now damp from the post-operative sweats.

'Carefully guide yourself into the chair, you have a wound and stitches so please take care by taking it slowly.'

Seeing Aurora's face told a thousand words, it must have been a success. Her smile and embrace was abundant in pure gratitude, as she whispered in his ear, 'we got it.' This was the news Noah had pined to hear since waking, and ever since he had met her. It was a revelation, it was possibility. He was relieved, as too, was Aurora. The first step in a quest had reached completion.

'Please ensure Noah takes bed rest for three days. We require that post-operative antibiotics be taken as a full course to prevent any infection,' the surgeon calmly instructed Aurora.

Having arrived home, Aurora got Noah comfortably settled and put together a warm Italian panini filled with roasted vegetables and goats cheese, accompanied by his favourite — a strong cappuccino. Memories of the nervous wait, the anxiety around the sedative and the nauseating wait in recovery quickly diminished as that smooth brew flowed expressly down his throat.

Aurora sat down quietly to read through the supplied outpatient protocols and the report written by the surgeon. She discovered that the operation had become largely more invasive than initially suggested. The surgeon had been forced beyond the stage of a simple extraction, needing to take tissue in the effort to locate enough of Noah's material to work with. A testicular biopsy had been required, and this would therefore, entail a longer period of physical recovery.

The first fluids Noah passed had brought discomfort. His body felt desecrated and brutalised — blood stained swabs and gauze pads served as an unsavoury reminder of what he had just encountered.

Two days passed with Noah taking complete bedrest and focusing on minimising any sudden or unnecessary movement, for the stitches felt tight and it was uncomfortable in almost any position. Sleep was challenging to sustain as the site of the surgery was generating intense throbbing and jagging sensations.

On the third day (not dissimilar to when Jesus was said to have emerged from the cave), positive news arrived — the quality was adequate, the volume acceptable however, the motility was largely questionable. This news brought the couple a step closer, it gave them hope. It did however, dictate that an alternate course of medical action would be required in order for ultimate success to be achieved; a completely scientific simulation, through in-vitro fertilisation, of the process our regular physiology allows — conception. They had hoped that a process appearing to be more natural would be available to them (the insertion of live semen directly into Aurora's womb), however, it was not. The issue of motility, determined that his seed needed the intervention of a scientist, it needed guidance within the confines of a petri dish.

This was bittersweet and there was the tendency to view what would be required as contrary to God's intended design. Further compromise would be required of the couple. It was certainly contrary to their pure and organic dispositions, and presented yet another moral dilemma. Both Noah and Aurora struggled to combat their own better knowing, as their preference was to always follow a natural course with regard to all things mind, body and spirit. These occurrences significantly threw otherwise innate preferences into complete disarray, delivering a sour and oppositional conflict between the choice to continue to pursue what they so longed for, and what they truly believed to be right on a holistic level. Limited for options and somewhat committed, the couple decided to forge ahead.

Alleviated by the confirmed success of his integral part in the process, Noah quickly turned his attention to the support of his love. The focus now needed to be shifted onto Aurora, and her emotional, mental and physical needs.

IV

LIFE IN THE PRESENCE OF DEATH

Aurora, faced her own personal internal conflicts with regard to the prescribed invasion of her body and what impact that would have on her reproductive integrity. For the experience of her role in the exchange had been clearly outlined by the fertility specialist as one that would be quite invasive. Much to her resistance, she had over the time since Noah's operation, undergone an unrelenting ambush of synthetic hormone therapy, with the objective of stimulating her ovaries to produce as many ovums as possible. Her aversion to this protocol was fundamentally driven by an innate opposition to the simulation of nature through contradictory mechanics and structures.

By design, the synthetic substance would hi-jack and manipulate her body through trickery, overriding its natural cycle (which was to produce only one egg each month). It was a paradox that she struggled to transcend. In order to facilitate what she dearly wanted, she faced a necessitation to continue the superimposition of artificially constructed methods, in contravention to the organic. Nonetheless, she had agreed to follow the program as outlined by the specialist.

Aurora adamantly disliked hypodermic needles and they had become a daily intruder into her abdomen along the journey she had now embarked on. Additionally, three further blood tests were scheduled, along with a final injection, in order to complete the cycle; one engineered to deceive her body into holding back, what would normally proceed into natural ovulation.

Not withstanding the prevalent considerations and moral conflict, the couple forthright in their vision held hope that through divine magnetism, the golden seed would pair with its destined match, a single ovum, manifesting a flowering emanation of their loving union.

Being it was the first time in her life that Aurora had needed to be admitted into hospital, she was grappling to process the intense apprehension. She wondered about the efficacy of the level of invasion she had agreed to undergo, ultimately deciding it be an inescapable sacrifice for a greater good to come of it. The thought of having to surrender to the anaesthetic delivered by yet another needle, had also filled her mind with worry. She knew not what to expect and had only Noah's recollection of his experiences to guide her as to what hers may be like. She had nursed him through two weeks of recovery, compassionately witnessing him move gingerly about their small apartment, toss and turn constantly through the night in vain attempts to find a comfortable position.

'Hi Aurora. I'm Ramish, your anaesthetist. I'll now administer the sedative. You'll be under for approximately three hours however, I'll be here to monitor you to make sure that everything will be fine,' he advised.

This brought her some much needed reassurance, alleviating some of the anxiety she'd been quelling with deep breaths during the wait. The door to the theatre closed, and the imminence of what was about to occur descended upon her. The team entrusted with the safeguarding and exploration of her body prepared to begin.

It signalled an end to one aspect of her journey, and gave rise to another. For over the time since Noah's procedure she had endured twenty-eight separate and memorable injections. These injections were mandated to be performed at home, which meant Noah, already managing his own dislike of needles, found himself, by default, the designated injector. The nurse had instructed him through a crash course in the handling and dispensation of the synthetic solution, suspended in glass vials, which had been packaged up into a take-home insulated bag. She had guided Noah through the storage requirements, preparation, safe delivery and disposal of the syringes housing the hormonal cocktail.

For fourteen long and arduous days, a systematic pin-cushioning of Aurora's abdomen occurred. In the end there were few new spots into which Noah could administer the shot. The remnant bruising of Noah's first clumsy attempt on the first night, was still apparent by day fourteen. It was a heavily emotional process, both for Noah and for his wife. He despised having to see her squirm, in apprehension of the needle's point piercing her skin, the seemingly slow rate at which the liquid was completely dispelled from the needle, and the consequent ghastly sensation of the needle being carefully drawn out. The frequency of this observably gruesome, yet necessary practice, had worn both of them down emotionally and mentally.

Aurora had suffered from discomfort, strange tingling sensations and a horrid bloating through the daily cycle of the two injections. Tears were shed each time as Noah would perform the ritualistic task, kindly giving support to his somewhat frightened patient. He had never handled a needle, and believed there was an art to it, a lightness of hand required. As far as he was concerned these administrations were better left to practitioners trained in such things. He had not the experience to masterfully minimise the discomfort however, night by night, improved in confidence and the application of the steady plunging action, whilst avoiding any deviating movements, the ones that make it more uncomfortable and the experience all the more unpleasant.

'We're all done, I'm sorry sweetheart...' Noah would relay empathically upon withdrawing the entire sharp from beneath her skin each time. He felt compelled to apologise. More or less from of a sense of guilt for what she was enduring as a consequence of his past actions. He took on full accountability and fought off immense bouts of guilt for it all. Noah felt responsible for what his love was having to endure through no fault nor shortcoming of her own. This was a burdensome aspect of the entire unwanted experience, for it was not meant to be this way, these last resorts presented confronting conflicts with their core beliefs.

'I'm so proud of you and respect you all the very more for your courageous spirit, understanding and for not judging our predicament. This is our time, we will be blessed with a baby, I know we will.'

As the nights passed, the sheer volume of medicine stored neatly in the fridge had diminished in size. It was a welcome reminder, and relief to both, that they had reached the penultimate stage in the journey — the removal of ovum from her body.

It was now Noah's turn to wait it out in the clinic. Proximity however, was on his side, as he was able to sit within earshot of the theatre in which his wife had been laid out.

As the cold sensation swept up her left arm Aurora focused her attention on positive thoughts and deep abdominal breathing. She called for her guides, her helpers, her maternal grandmother Lois, and her higher self, asking for protection during the time she would be 'out.'

Noah, sat patiently in wait, sensing a powerful energy circulating throughout the clinic. The same three guides that had worked in the capacity of guardians during his procedure, had positioned themselves strategically in the operating room overseeing Aurora. Having refined a natural ability to acutely perceive of energy fields, Noah strongly intuited another prominent energetic signature. His higher sensory perception guided him towards the likelihood of the presence of a particular group of guides shared by the couple, three Musketeers.

The Musketeers had made themselves known to Noah and Aurora several years back, bringing prophetic insight and a promise to fulfil a debt from a past life. They had not relayed what the couple had done for them to have earned the 'favour' however, the couple had decided that the blessing of a child be an appropriate and equalising gesture in return.

The clock on the wall had taken two full revolutions of its face, and sometime into the third hour the surgeon appeared. Whilst being conscious not to jump on the weary professional, Noah politely gestured with a view to gleaning an insight into his wife's wellbeing.

'She's doing fine. We were able to retrieve twelve eggs. All going well, we'll be able to schedule a transfer five days from now.'

The surgeon's explanation pleased both Noah and his mother, Pamela, who had made the trip over the seas to be of support to her only son and daughter-in-law.

'Do you think she's going to be alright to continue on with the process so soon? After all the medication and now this?' Pamela critically enquired of the nurse, herself carrying an earnest mistrust of the foreign medical institution bombarding her son's wife with sequentially invasive interventions. She had witnessed all but just two of the home injections, placing her own fears and concerns aside, in order to lend support to the ones she loved most.

'The transfer is a simple procedure, there is nothing invasive about this part of the process,' the nurse matter of factly stated.

Aurora's wait in the recovery area took a while longer than it had for Noah, for Aurora's body already bruised, pricked and depleted, had just endured another great physical, psychological and spiritual challenge. The recovery time entailed sleep and more sleep. The grogginess brought on deep bursts of vivid dreaming, something for which she was accustomed. She dreamed deeply shifting her consciousness into a future time where she frolicked, dancing upon the grassy hillside sprawling with sunflowers, viewing the emblazoned horizon holding hands with her cherished one. There was no sense of gender, for the distinction between boy or girl was of no consequence. Aurora had long played the role as 'Keeper of the Children,' and was now thrust into the realm of personal destiny, as she stood on the precipice of her divine purpose — to become mother.

Having woken in recovery and been transported back to Noah in the waiting room, the doctor relayed that the fertilisation process would commence immediately and confirmed that the transfer procedure would be set down for five days from then.

Aurora cast her mind forward five days ahead to the final stage — the implantation of their child, in microscopic life form, into her womb. A mixture of excitement and resignation coursed through her spirit. She felt relieved, yet defeated, battered, prodded and probed. She didn't feel there was adequate time available to build up her energy reserves for this next stage — the process felt rushed, unnatural and out of divine timing. Her internals had suffered trauma, the bloating had not subsided, she was tired and had become displeased with the loss of sovereignty over her own body.

The doctor proceeded to prescribe a course in antibiotics to prevent infection, something that Aurora had much resistance in adhering to, as she was well aware of the adverse effects they have on the body. Compounding this, was the directive that she inflict her body with yet more artificial substances. Whilst not anywhere near as distasteful as the endless subjugation to the hypodermics, the requirement now was the introduction of additional hormones to prepare her 'house' for the embryo's arrival. A sludgy synthetic concoction was prescribed, once again to be dutifully doctored by Noah.

The end in the long turbulent road had drawn nearer, one along which they had run the gamut of emotional highs and lows. What was to follow would be a culmination; the transfer of their creation in embryonic form, into her loving womb.

All the while, the guides, along with the Musketeers, stood guard in the laboratory, each performing a specific role, some in the karmic, past-life favour to be returned.

The young embryologist carefully moved the ovums, all twelve, into the space where the genetic alchemy was to be performed. The Musketeers, entrusted with assuring that the two precious materials be divinely unified, assembled. One assumed an officious and extremely serious posture before the cabinet where the father's seed lay in waiting, frozen in time. The other two, one slightly smaller in stature, stationed themselves in the other section where the mother's divinity was marked, secured and stored. Their posturing took a trusting, yet protective presence. They were to see to it, that the genetic matter be treated with integrity, and that the alchemical union be approached with great finesse and mindfulness. Their primary objective was to course the best of selections, by guiding the trained hands of the embryologist toward the ovums displaying the most optimum potential — the ones which emanated significantly more radiant light, golden in nature.

As the embryologist meticulously prepared the trays the Musketeers checked and double checked that all was in place. They had taken all precaution in their valiant efforts to repay the debt from many lifetimes prior, making alterations to the sequence of the specimens in order for the ideal fertilisation to take place. They selected eight ovums that they had scanned for ideal expression, ordering them in such a way so as to attract the embryologist to them. She had a sense of something present in the room and had even questioned whether items had been moved, even renumbered.

Eight eggs successfully fertilised. It was the eventual culmination of powerful physical, and non-physical collaboration propelled by pure intention, that characterised this moment. For Noah and Aurora the miracle of life had been achieved, they stood at the dawning moment in the realisation of their dream.

Aurora struggled mentally and physically with the pressure that the next phase was to bring — motherhood. She had looked forward to being fully present and able, to enjoy the pregnancy, their fruit of miracles, but now found herself bedridden with overwhelming fatigue. In contrast to the gratitude she held, she had grown irritated, frustrated and burdened by the weight now on her shoulders. She disliked the pressure to perform, requesting that she transcend physical fatigue, and carry her starseed into existence. She felt inadequately prepared and rushed into adhering to the schedule that placed, in such proximity, a sequence of such emotionally demanding experiences. She mused over the uncertainty. Her intuition was to postpone, but part of her wanted to ride the momentum, to fight one last chapter in her sacred quest to be ordained as the 'keeper' of her own child, as mother.

But the predominantly fatigued state of being brought on grave thoughts of ironic failure.

'Am I meant to mother in this life?'

'Will this happen for us?'

She traced over dark thoughts of vacancy and despair. Her role in this play was by virtue of his shortcomings, for whilst her body had never brought a child into the world, her reproductive system operated in harmony as it should. She had by default, taken a lead role in an otherwise, unnecessary play.

Continual requests to the universe through affirmation, pleas to the aether, and to anyone in the higher realms listening, had left the couple unfulfilled for many years. A deep sense of paranoia had crept into Noah's mind too. He questioned if, and when this blessing was to be bestowed, only to be further compounded by the several weeks riddled with emotional turmoil, married with ethically challenging decisions to overcome.

When something that one so deeply desires labours in its ability to manifest, the level of hope, belief and conviction demanded of an individual increases significantly. But some things manifest quietly, slowly and invisibly. Just as the bamboo plant spends some fifteen years amassing its energy beneath the level of the ground, only to one day burst forth into existence growing with grandiose and rapid speed, life's manifestations often occur shrouded in the same level of intrigue.

The day had come for the divinely guarded golden potential to be placed inside of her womb. Her inner knowing resounded in the truth that it was not the ideal circumstance, yet her commitment required that she march onward. She had figured that deliverance had moved closer, so any postponement would seem pointless, it would be postponing the inevitable for which they had already waited long enough.

Noah took the same position on the chair in the waiting room of the clinic, just as he had only days prior. Once again he fretted and agonised over the welfare of his love, hoping that she would be alright. He spent his time praying that she would emerge from the room carrying that golden light, that had not yet decided to embrace their world, until now.

Noah himself had also diminished in his overall state of wellbeing, the antibiotics depleting his body and placing his immune system under pressure. He had processed significant concerns fending off looping thoughts of post-operative complications and possible infection.

To his delight Aurora emerged from the room appearing unphased following a refreshingly non-invasive procedure.

It was done. The finest choice had been placed up high on the left of Aurora's womb. Mother and child, in blastocyst phase, five days into life, were now one. Noah could hardly contain his emotion. He gently pulled Aurora close whispering, '...we have our precious treasure now.'

Noah felt a great sense of relief, he had finally been able to give her what he had always envisioned. He had felt hopelessly damned by his past, he hadn't the insight as to what the future would bring; more children to a different wife was not something he ever considered. But life changes, it can change in an instant, in this forever evolving universe.

His life had just taken another transformative leap, it was now a time signifying the fulfilment of a very dear and heavy desire. It marked the closure to that old and torrid set of fears, which had conceived of a barren future. Decaying his mental health, it had developed into perhaps his greatest fear, for which he would, on a daily basis, traumatise himself through the apportioning of blame.

Over the next couple of days any internal sensations, or sense of life force flowing through Aurora's body were quickly and excitedly relayed to Noah. Both definitely felt the new energy projecting from her body and encapsulating their space. It was a truly golden and illuminating source energy. There was a warmth and a sense of light, of energy centred around her second chakra, where the associated external layer still exhibited small dark puncture marks. This surprised Aurora, as she had summated that her body would likely not be able to hold the pregnancy.

Having navigated a taxing, frustrating and fruitless journey to reach this point in time (when the dream of a child appeared imminent to be blessed upon them), she committed to taking command of any negativity, as this represented the final frontier, the last remaining hope. Dedicating herself to the mastery of her own mind, she vowed to adhere to her characteristically optimistic mindset, as much as she couldn't feel adequate reason to. Her decision was to let go, dispel the fear and negativity, and invariably surrender to the divine plan.

The fertility specialist had adamantly warned the couple against becoming overly optimistic, given the relative ratios and variables involved which would dictate success, or otherwise. Aurora, knowing full well how she felt, had a reluctance to announce herself as pregnant, however, Noah succumbed somewhat to blind optimism and an inappropriate level of expectation ignoring the advice. He could not bear to even conceive of the embryo not holding, that Aurora's body was understandably not ready physically or spiritually, nor that it may not be the divine time. As such, he hastily implied to his mother that it was all an assured success, as if believing that by his own will, he could dictate that ultimate success be assured. Telling someone of success made it feel real, reckoned and actualised. It pronounced an end to a period of his life; a death of the old.

V

TRANSFORMATION GESTATES
THROUGH AWARENESS

*"If you don't heal the wounds of the past,
          then you'll bleed all over your future."*

For Noah, the prospect of once again becoming a father triggered the opening of a passage in synchronous time, where he would be compelled to unpack, and face the accumulated trauma housed in his pain body, where the state of mental, and emotional disease had lodged. The impending news of a pregnancy served to bring memories of his son flooding back. There were contrasting moments, some where he positively reminisced, and others where he felt the sadness, that he'd till now, failed to reconcile. Sadness, pain and guilt can take years to work through, to acknowledge, process and collapse, but grief's visceral tentacle can remain attached for longer. The guilt had become resoundingly cruel in its power to occupy his mind and sabotage his progress, despite his best efforts in clearing it out by means of affirmation, meditation and healing.

As a man and a father, he sought not to replace what had been lost, in order to heal these wounds. His motivating intention was to celebrate his love, and to once again experience the miracle of creation, and of being a father to Aurora's child. It was from within this deepest desire, that the pure unadulterated want, for the successful transfer of their genetic union, originated.

Noah was a man who naturally embodied feminine principles, there was a synergy to his energetic disposition. For he had as much acted in the capacity of a mother, as he had a father, to his son. He nurtured him through his formative years, the all-important ones, from birth to seven. He had been afforded enough time with which to impart his view of the world, of life, and of what he perceived as meaningful. He parented with the loving wisdom of the maternal, and fathered with his courageous warrior spirit.

It had taken miraculous courage, faith and time in holistic self-analysis to take the next step on his path, and to dissolve the marriage to his former wife. Whilst this mammoth change in course delivered him to the freedom needed to discover himself, it had likewise, blossomed burdensome pain, resulting in a heartbreaking disconnect which perpetrated thickly rooted guilt. The gravity of this cross to bear weighed heavily upon his days. This beast of burden, governed by the decisions of the past, rendered him often be-swept with tears descending down his cheek, verbalising the identifiable tones of grief, and that gut-wrenching sadness.

He had long dwelled over this pain, the pain he had presumed to have inflicted on his son. The guilt associated with the perceived damage he had orchestrated through his actions, supercharged dire concern for his son's future.

Gone were the days of full-time fatherhood; even the days of being a casual one had dissipated into the void. Communication had become a futile exercise, by virtue of his child being coerced into making a choice not to have any contact with him whatsoever. There were no short interludes over the phone, nor long days spent in the sunshine at the park. There wasn't even the awareness of his son's whereabouts, his likes and dislikes or his successes and failures.

Noah felt undeserving of these consequences that had resulted from the choice he heartfully knew was the rightful one. How could no longer wanting to be married to a particular person, equate to not wanting to father anymore — *it didn't*. He had unselfishly sacrificed himself for too long, and when that journey came to its crossroad, he lacked the foresight to determine that the good, would also come with a brewing dose of the bad. Thus, when hearts were broken, dreams were shattered and promises unkept, his role was forsaken and life ceased to serve justice.

His mind cast itself back in recollection of times before when he had fathered, and how much joy it had brought into his experience of life. Of how he deeply loved and cherished playing with his dear little boy. Whilst he had taken on newer and broader perspectives in the context of life and valuable learnings from this heavy pain, the distance between him and his child seemed insurmountable. Too many potential moments, days, weeks and years, were being lost in the sands of time, never to be returned, and this lacerated him emotionally.

Noah unbeknownst to him, had arrived at a critical juncture on the timeline, a point of profound discovery in his life. For what he was on the verge of unearthing, was something that he could have never rightly imagined, nor expected. It was to be the moment when the pain, guilt, sadness and fear surrounding his child's welfare, would find resolution.

'I wonder how James faired in the final year of high school?' Noah posed the question whilst reclined on the sofa.

The question catapulted him through a myriad of confused thoughts and feverish emotion, with an air of intense futility. For he lacked a clear avenue through which he'd be able to gain the information he sought. How was he to find out without an open line of communication with the boy, now a man? His mother would surely not be interested in gratifying him with a response to such queries; her anger and judgement of Noah's betrayal was still too entrenched.

'Okay, so I have no reliable means of finding out this information, I'm not going to dignify a message that is unlikely to be acknowledged in reply, and certainly not going to suffer the embarrassment of contacting the school,' Noah self-assessing and admitting that he didn't like the idea of being given the run around by a school who wouldn't trust he was entitled to such personal information. For they had never met him, and his boy had for some time been under the parental guidance of a new father figure; a new partner to his ex-wife.

Sitting bolt upright on the edge of the sofa, whilst Aurora still rested her tired body, Noah followed various streams, of what he assumed would be fruitless enquiry. Despite this, he searched with a vigour, like a man that had been possessed with the thirst for knowledge, and an underlying supposition of a man on the precipice of a breakthrough. Noah hoped as he traversed all relevant and available avenues, that the news he would find would be news of success. For if the boy had of avoided complete failure, even achieved something, then Noah expected that this indeed would denote the time for him to alleviate himself of layers of guilt and fear, around what had transpired.

Noah inadvertently discovered the most unexpected, yet transcendently moving news that he could have possibly uncovered. His son was victorious! In relation to his education, James had flourished in Noah's absence and attained a level of perfection that was hardly believable. It took numerous glances, double-checking, cross-checking and even confirmation through Aurora's eyes, that the results he was seeing, were in fact true.

James had trumped his education. There were perfect scores, scattered amongst near perfect scores, and most notably, a choice of subjects mirroring those undertaken by Noah during his senior education. He had achieved a perfect set of five subject awards and thus been awarded the title, Valedictorian.

The tears poured down Noah's face, he howled in exultation of his boy's demonstrated mastery amidst challenging circumstance, and for the drive in overcoming, what Noah worried was, a terminal blow to his heart inflicted by his departure.

'I cannot believe what I have just seen, it's incredible. He did so well, his achievements are outstanding. He's so smart, he always was. I worried so much whether or not he would regain the stability, the focus, and build the strength and happiness to accomplish great things without me.'

Noah had a tendency to take full responsibility for what he considered to be ruining his son's childhood. He had perceived his actions could have wounded James' spirit, stifled his obvious talent and adversely affected his future development.

'I'm so glad that he applied himself so positively.'

Noah's relief was overwhelming, a weight lifted from his shoulders. It was such profound news to hear after six years of complete disconnection. Much of the rooted guilt and fear around the boy's wellbeing and future, passed away into the aether, at that moment, right there and then. It was released, and it released Noah.

The success represented validation in the choices Noah had made, which at the time, had been branded selfish and irresponsible. All he had wished for was the freedom to pursue what his heart told him, with that freedom coming at as little cost to others as possible. He had not enjoyed breaking his son's heart, in order to follow the fulfilment of his own.

Noah swiftly called his mother Pamela and announced the brilliant news. Her disbelief obvious, Pamela found herself asking Noah multiple times how he discovered the information and whether it had been authenticated. Such was the level of achievement, she bellowed out across her kitchen towards the reading room where her husband Keith was catching up on matters of global finance.

'Keith! James achieved a perfect score in his final year of school! How marvellous is that?' Pamela boasted.

Not withstanding the perfection achieved by the boy, came a greater manifestation of irony in their proposed vocational paths. The boy James, was to become James the lawyer, the solicitor, the barrister and perhaps even James the judge. His score entitled him a place in the most prestigious law school in the city. The scores had reminded

Noah of his failure to reach law school, the dream he had conjured to be his own during his time scaling the rungs of the educational ladder. This dream remained unfulfilled. But now, the boy was set to not only fulfil this dream, but perhaps assume greatness.

The synchronicity in the subject choices that had been undertaken by James activated pivotal connections in Noah's mind. Not only had the boy achieved better results than that of his father, he had also performed a feat thought impossible — a perfect English score. This was a rare occurrence under the standardised system of grading; it was a miraculous expression of talent and mastery in language. There were major confirmations and fundamental realisations in his son's demonstrated talent for the written word.

Noah's admiration for his son's intellect had synchronously reminded him of one of his own natural talents — which was to write. He fairly assessed that in all likelihood, these abilities had been passed through his ancestral line, given English was also his forte.

'If James writes so well, then I remember now, so can I, we are father and son', he thought.

This was a moment of divine singular awareness and harmony through interpreted meaning. It was a significant activation.

'He didn't just do okay, he absolutely, positively excelled,' Noah proclaimed to Aurora, who whilst diminished in energy and recovering from all the procedures, shared his happiness in hearing the news.

'I need to acknowledge this.'

Noah felt compelled to contact the boy and tell him how proud he was, despite expecting that the acknowledgment would be unwanted. There was a respect for him as a human being.

'I must make contact with him. His achievements are tremendous to say the least. I want to pay respect to his dedication and ability to overcome the instability and the obstacles he must have faced over the years. Even if he doesn't get the message, read it or even reply, which I don't expect he will, it's important he knows that I'm just so immensely proud of him.'

Noah continued his emotional outpourings, with peaks of sheer relief, beautiful relief. The great love one has for a son burned brightly, however, without the overshadowing clouds that darkened recent fatherhood.

'I'm sending a message, do you think that it's okay?'

Often Noah liked to engage Aurora's opinion as to the integrity of his motivations and the appropriateness of his actions in life. She presented a virtuous, mature, empathetic and balanced view, so was a good confidante to have in ensuring mindful, conscious and loving decisions were made across the many aspects in the navigation of life.

'Yes, I think this requires your acknowledgement and irrespective of whether or not he chooses to respond, you should contact him.'

Noah sent the message and spent many hours crying volumes of happy tears for the happiness he felt.

He pondered what he had just witnessed. For Noah, the revelations that had come with the news of James' achievement, served to provide him with clearer insights;

deeper insights into the very nature of his own set of spiritual challenges that stood in the way of reaching his highest expression. It allowed Noah to better identify that in fact, the dissolution of his parents marriage had not adversely effected his development either, as many commonly and stereotypically are led to believe; that personal fragmentation is simply summated as being the product of a broken home. For Noah too had flourished through that experience. The accomplishments of his son thus, delivered him with an insight into exactly what his traumas were, and what they weren't. This was an invaluable byproduct of his discovery, as one can't resolve that which is not able to be clearly identified.

Two days passed with no response from his son; Noah hadn't expected one, it wasn't the motivation for the message — acknowledgement was the driver.

Aurora had made her best efforts to remain positive and calm for the embryo to take residence within her, and seat itself upon her womb for the nine month journey into outwardly physical existence.

The antibiotics prescribed by the doctor had been surreptitiously thrown out three days into the course. Aurora's body had rejected any further foreign substances or interventions. Her body relaying to her, through the voice of symptom, that it preferred it not be interfered with, and allowed time to rejuvenate. Her spirit too, longed for a break from the arduous process that they had embarked on — she was spiritually fatigued.

Aurora had witnessed her thoughts, her emotional state and her essence, her prana diminish in strength. She knew intuitively that her body was not in the optimal state for a successful carriage. Her physical fragility, the expression of a railroaded patient, moving from one unenviable process to another. The culmination of which was the expectation of her body to carry a child to birth, under the most testing of circumstances.

Then the news came.

The divine timings lost synchronisation with the material realm. By no virtue of positive affirmation, nor solemn prayer, was there to be success in this moment. The soul choosing not to assign itself to imminent habitation, preferring to remain in stasis, waiting for the synchronous opportunity to become available in a time yet to come. Perhaps a time when the couple's frequency and level of embodiment was higher, when Aurora would be able energetically, to hold the spirit's high codings and frequency.

'Not pregnant!'

The painfully stark verdict delivered unemotionally by the doctor agitated Noah.

'How can she deliver news like that with such detachment and lack of compassion?'

'Unbelievable. No empathy whatsoever!' Aurora verbalising disgust in the manner in which the medical profession had been trained to detach from all emotion in the course of their work.

It's difficult to remain positive, balanced and in control of one's own faculties when life defining expectations are smattered in an instant. It's when it feels like the darkness has come calling for you, and you alone.

This was not what Noah had envisaged, for they were on the final stretch on their passage to parenthood. For Aurora it was a saddening reflection of a reality she had already resigned herself to. She knew the embryo had ceased its development and that the desired manifestation of their love was to be delayed to a later date on the timelines.

Noah also had to be honest with himself, he had no longer felt the presence of the same life force energy. He recollected how in the first four days following transfer, he *had* felt it. He had felt life and the presence of their child growing tenderly within his beloved's womb.

Needing to place his most intense desires to one side, he had reconciled himself to the fact that his wife was not fairly prepared for motherhood. This was an easier cross to bear now, as it was not a matter of *if* they could expect to enjoy parenthood, but a matter of *when*. For both, this was far more than a subtle distinction — it was everything. A dark reflective object had been lifted away to reveal the sun's liberating rays. It denoted an end to a period of debilitating paranoia and unsureness for the future.

For Aurora, the mere fact that the mountainous task of capturing her love's seed had been fortuned was an emotional climax in itself. The expectation placed upon her to hold the pregnancy, surpassed what was appropriate and divinely harmonic. The undue pressure to continue the journey onward, playing out the robust patient able to transit into pregnancy then onto motherhood, rationalised this fork in the road. Spiritually she needed respite, restoration, renewal and resurrection.

This was not something she had willingly shared with her partner. He possessed his own deep drivers. As having endured the decade long shadow of sterility, a failed pregnancy was not an outcome Noah was willing to entertain. The level of affliction paled in significance with the emotional matter that Aurora fought prominently within her consciousness.

'I want to share with you that I knew my body and my being was not ready to take a baby to full term. It has been too much for me in quick succession. I feel my body needs a break, to heal the internal stitches, to detoxify the remnant hormones, the synthetic trickeries and the abhorrent antibiotics,' Aurora confessed languidly.

'I feel terrible. I want at least two monthly cycles so my system may once again feel strong. I want to be ready and enjoy this, not be rushed, with no time to take stock and acclimatise to the fact that we can now have a child. We weren't to know this before, now we can be at ease, we have the choice to try again whenever we choose.'

Aurora's monologue only confirmed what Noah had sensed to be the case in relation to her state of mind, emotional durability and overall wellbeing. It had been over four weeks of roller-coasting confrontations contrasted by the unveiling of emotionally supercharged revelations.

The couple returned home, ordered in Thai deciding to bond and spend time comfortably in their own space together. They needed a period of quality alone time in each other's presence, as they were both justifiably emotional, still processing the news. Having enjoyed the variety of flavoursome dishes, Noah had an idea to distract themselves from what had just transpired, and inject some playful fun into the evening.

'Let's play a video game!"

He jumped to retrieve the gaming unit from the suitcase stored away. They rarely chose to interface with such things, and thus, hadn't considered playing it for well over seven years, since James visited last. The console offering all manner of virtual contests had been purchased for him, as he was a gifted strategist.

'This reminds me so much of James. He was so advanced in terms of his ability to accomplish feats previously unheard of in a boy his age. He would complete entire games in two days you know!'

Noah enjoyed reminiscing these times, and playing the console offered some connection back into them. It was a glimpse into the time when James was prominent in his life, and stayed over on weekends; when he could still feel the warmth of James' heart in physical embrace. Despite Noah's awareness that the higher realm connections were always strong and unbreakable, he missed the physical presence.

There was now a new capacity with which to once again experience joyful memory, without the predictable onslaught of sadness, pain and guilt, as had been the case in years past. It was a refreshed perspective laying its foundation in the positive, as opposed to the negative. He felt free from the emotional turbulence and rather uplifted instead. Noah welcomed this new found ability to recollect these times without the gut-wrenching angst and worry; as those shackles that bound had been loosened off, somewhat. The musings of his negative ego and his subconscious had dissipated in their taunting voices, leaving only loving feelings and heart based memories on which to reflect.

In a moment of gaming genius Noah emulated the boy — he circumvented the traps, blocked the hammers, climbed the walls, avoided the pitfalls, leaped over the nets, overcame the invaders and ceremoniously captured the flag atop the mountain in the final challenge of the game. He stood victorious just as the boy had.

VI

THE SPIRITUAL FLU

From the outside, one may be inclined to assume that the simple action of relocating away from the big city, to a lush tropical island, would serve to quickly melt one's worries away with the sun. To some extent many of Noah's displeasures had been alleviated through this change from concrete to jungle, but not to the extent that he aspired to in order to embody the true inner peace and fulfillment he knew was possible for him. The all new environment had though, provided a fresh, stimulating and appropriately chosen platform, from which Noah could reset, deconstruct, rebuild and move closer towards the attainment of the transformation he sought.

He had set out to sea, a fragmented navigator at the helm of his human vessel, sailing unchartered waters toward a destination somewhere on the vast horizon. He had spent his life in partial disillusion, scooting across this ravaging ocean in this foreign and broken world, this paradise lost. But now here he was, moored in a happier port — dearly loved, married, secure, supported and stable. Nonetheless, he found himself plunged into a real funk, a depressive state of being that he'd experienced many times before. The difference was that this time it carried an overwhelmingly more determining energy as if perhaps, the confrontation with his shadow had reached its climax, as though this was to be the storm that he would not out-sail.

Since the invasive operation and the disappointment of the failed pregnancy, Noah had lost his otherwise healthy appetite, becoming somewhat nutritionally apathetic. Throughout the preceding months, they had removed animal products, particularly meat, from both their diets. They were aware of the crude practices adopted in modern industrialised meat production — the proliferation of cruelty, the use of antibiotics, growth hormones in addition to inorganic feed and the inhumane conditions for the livestock. Conditions that encompassed mistreatment, the experience of fear, confinement and a myriad of other unnatural interventions.

Whilst this innately guided shift appeared to be one in favour of veganism, it was in fact a decision based not upon the belief that these products ought be removed from their diet, but more so that they be guaranteed of its integrity and quality. Their opinion was also that one of the rarely identified consequences of mass meat production, was that the meat itself carried a very low vibration, due to the animals being subjected to such a traumatic existence — and they firmly believed that this energetic signature would be transmitted into their bodies upon eating it.

As such, Noah and Aurora required assurances that their meat be pasture-raised or wild caught, fed a natural diet, free of GMOs, hormones and any other toxic constituents. In their view, this would thereby guarantee the health and welfare of the animals, as well as the environment, which would consequently translate into an optimum nutritional profile for them as the consumers. However, given their foreign residence where language posed a barrier, the couple struggled to source an ethical supplier, and thus, chose to boycott the purchase of any animal products, until which time they were able to secure one that met their justifiably valid criteria.

Likewise, both Noah and Aurora were skeptical in relation to the movement towards this nutritional trend that had swept across the world. Reading between the lines, both had drawn the conclusion that there was another multi-national conspiracy at play. It was a global agenda which, under the umbrella of climate change, conveniently utilised this rationale as justification in order to meet its objectives. Through a set of multi-faceted strategies it sought to create a new industry producing synthetic GMO meat substitutes generating higher profits. This in turn would decimate the traditional farming industry by driving established farmers from the land, having succumbed to financial collapse, thereby with no other choice but to remove their animals from natural pastures (a key component in a healthy planetary ecosystem). This strategy was geared to allow the ruling class to reclaim the land inexpensively and also increase the prevalence of colossal mono-crops that were already wreaking havoc upon the planet. Furthermore, this agenda had been purposed to further orchestrate poor health in humans, who were already over fed and under-nourished. Instead of reconfiguring a broken system through the promotion of sustainable bio-dynamic practices, the vilification of meat generally served to guide the relative state of collective health, further toward sickness — as organic, ethically raised animal produce carries bio-available nutrients and essential amino acids crucial for human development.

As a result, Noah had lost weight and was battling with constant fatigue, regularly needing to nap in the afternoon.

Energetically, he wasn't doing well at all. It was indicative and symptomatic of the slow downward spiral into general entropy, confusion about life and compromised immunity — this despite all the progress and discoveries highlighting the past weeks.

The decay of the old had now made manifest outwardly. This less than desirable state of physical, mental and emotional health had become observable through Noah's skin, the largest organ in the human body. When the skin develops a rash, boils, pimples and alike, its function is to provide a sign which is symptomatic of an underlying cause; such appearances are for the purpose of communicating that something within the body is either depleted, deficient or malfunctioning.

His skin had deteriorated, which was alarming as he had always enjoyed a good complexion and looked relatively youthful considering his age. The skin covering his legs was cracked, irritated, itchy and devoid of life. He observed them as scaly, not unlike that of snake skin. This dryness presenting on the outer, had become a source of frustration, alerting him to something untoward. It was symbolic of the life sustaining moisture having been gradually droughted from his body, rendering his appearance to that of an arid desert.

Further compounding the rare skin trouble, the apathy around food, the unrequited dream of again becoming a father, and the ongoing search to uncover his divine purpose, was the anguish of insomnia. For the first time in his life, he nightly faced the inability to sleep, which fast became an annoying monkey on his back.

For some two months it had been the same repetitive nightly cycle showcasing restlessness and lack of quality sleep. He would turn in at 9:00pm only to wake at midnight; expecting it to be morning, he'd rise, check the time and then try to reset himself. He requested of his guides, guardian angels and those passed that were dear to him, that he be taken in their arms and carried off into an extended break from the monotony and agony.

Lack of sleep adversely effects your everyday level of wellbeing, and furthermore, periods of insomnia are torturous to the mind. After a while, the restless and disjointed routine breaks you. One can end up completely giving up on the expectation of a good night's sleep, succumbing to past experience and thus preempting the same future. It becomes a self-inflicted, self-fulfilling prophecy.

'I'm not going to be able to sleep, I didn't last night and when I did, I woke only a few hours later,' Noah regularly frustrated.

Noah struggled with the exasperation of this even more, as throughout the night, if he was unable to sleep, there was nowhere to disappear to in the thirty-three square metre apartment. Noah, a considerate man, refused to turn on any lights, as this would inevitably disturb Aurora. Instead, he'd stumble around in the dark, trying not to create any disturbance — but you know what happens when you try too hard not to make any noise; you, as if by some cruel irony, end up inadvertently making the noises that wake people.

Noah hadn't slept through the night in a long while. The days all blended to a point where it didn't matter so much what time it was, or whether it was day or night. Sleep was short and inconsistent. The only place where he could be up and minimise disturbance, was out on the balcony. He spent hours on end, through the onerous nights, out there staring into space. These hours, he came to realise, were specifically designed for him to quietly ponder. It was time to wade through the deepest depths of his psyche. He had grown weary to the constant feelings of being personally unfulfilled, of not knowing who he was, or what potential this life contained for him.

Out on the confines of the balcony, Noah sat in silent observation of his life, once again.

'I've committed to the work of the spirit. I've strived to reach the gateway of spiritual liberation, been brave and persistent enough to stick out the fight until that time came. I dedicate to walking a virtuous and righteous path. I respect my body, I meditate, I cleanse myself with healing frequencies, practice daily yoga and have fostered a positive mindset. I consider myself to be both holistic and optimistic, but why am I still tormented? Why don't I feel whole?'

Noah heard a voice.

'Can't you sleep again? What time is it?' asked Aurora.

She was highly attuned for sensing energetic disturbances, therefore, often knew when Noah had silently removed himself from the bed.

'I'm alright. I'm just going to stay up, and sit out here, okay?' Noah answered through the gap in the door to the balcony.

He went on lamenting under the stars — 'I've got a beautiful partner whom I dearly love, I have money, I have shelter, food and nothing in particular to worry about. I'm not terminal with disease and I live in the tropics; what do I have to be glum over? Why can't I pull myself together, experience inner peace and enjoy life to its fullest? I don't understand why I feel this way, the boredom, the despondence and disconnect within myself. I'm so tired of feeling dull and living with this. I need to know my purpose and my mission in life in order to feel whole.'

A shadow had attained dominance over his soul, overlaying itself, spreading and multiplying over his life, and the lifetimes prior to that. Hopeful though, had he always been, that the dawn would eventually come, emancipating him into union and peace. A time where he would joyously live as liberated from this bondage, as the child born again. He had become a victim to himself, to his unfolding fate and to his experiences. This pained him greatly as all he longed for, is what we all long for — to be "...*the master of his fate and the captain of his soul.*"

The monotonous sleep deprivation continued. It was in the early hours of the morning on a Thursday, May 30th, and he had once again woken prematurely. In a concerted effort to break the cycle, this time he decided to stay in bed and return to sleep state. After repeating personal affirmations of gratitude for his blessings in life and giving thanks to his guardian angels, guides and to the universe, he managed to resume his slumber.

Noah rose at dawn with a thumping headache and an undeniable awareness that he was alarmingly ill. He assessed relatively quickly that he wasn't fit for work; he was accustomed to listening to his body. The fact that he wasn't going to be able to make the work commitments set for that day just didn't matter in the slightest. He didn't care, he was depleted and weak; he hadn't even the urge for coffee and to him this spoke volumes of his impending predicament.

Aurora feeling not too dissimilar, had decided that she would instead martyr herself and attempt to fulfil their commitments. She deemed it preferable not to have to deal with any confrontation that would inevitably come if both of them were to call in sick, particularly as they had taken time off to recover from the surgeries. Noah protested, insisting Aurora stay home, rest and sleep it off. This was out of concern for her welfare, as she had historically put the needs of others before her own, much to her own detriment. However, being the strong spirit she was, she ignored Noah's advice, deciding to pull herself together and go.

Noah was not feeling at all well and was already envisaging the worst, particularly as he normally enjoyed consistently good health, free of illness. He wondered if Aurora was feeling anything close to what he was? If so, she must have regretted going into work.

He had become increasingly confounded by the nature of the sickness, largely due to the dizziness, nausea, body aches and disconcerting crawling sensation under his skin. He lay there collating the list of symptoms that continued to accumulate, now including ringing in the ears and looping paranoid thoughts. He grappled with his tendency to worry and over-think, to feel isolated and alone without the capacity to look after himself. Despite this, he managed to get back to sleep during the time Aurora was out working.

Aurora walked back through the door and slumped straight into bed. It was only 11:22am (there were those numbers again, appearing so synergistically when either would check the time). She admitted that going into work, even just for that hour, that one class, had made her so much worse; the headache was now a thunderous migraine.

Whenever either of the two were sick, which had only occurred twice and never at the same time, Noah would feel it earlier than Aurora. This time both were knocked out cold — fever, sweats, diarrhoea, nausea, mental fog, uncontrollable fits of tears, headache, lower back tenderness and an all-encompassing feeling of weakness. Accompanying all of this was an unnervingly bulging pressure where the pineal gland sits, deep in the brain. This had given both of them an insight into the more than physical nature of events. They felt as though what was taking place, held deep significance on a metaphysical level; as much as the physical symptoms demanded their undivided attention.

Neither were in any condition to get up, or leave the room, to see anyone, to speak, or even to walk. Even the trip to the bathroom felt like a major ordeal. There was only the surrendered stillness in the respite of the wet sheet below their itching spines, and two minds running wild on the waves of fever. There wasn't any food prepared and they hadn't much of anything left (not that this mattered yet as they had no appetite whatsoever). As neither were well enough to provide any support to the other, panic had quickly set in. The imminent concerns became how they would get water when it ran out.

Now in the clutches of the *Flu's* outward manifestation they both slept on and off, only capable of feeling into their bodies. Both were awaiting some kind of epiphany, anything that would explain what it was that was causing such suffering. When one's wellbeing is careering downhill it's not difficult to convince yourself of a diabolical diagnosis bearing an even more sinister prognosis.

'Do we have Dengue fever? Is this diet related? Or could it be that we're run down and detoxing the remnants of the chemicals and medications from our procedures?'

Given what they knew of the world, having researched the state of reality studiously for many years, many possibilities flowed between them — from sinister tropical diseases through to classified black op technology.

'What if it's severe radiation poisoning from exposure to millimetre waves? Or a parasitic infestation from the transmission of an advanced bio-weapon?'

All the unknowns brought panic. It's a quiet and personal panic that goes with self-observation under duress; you martyr yourself to your own mind in these times. However, unbeknownst to them, they were undergoing an organic and timely kundalini activation, characterised by a physical purge. It was a manifest expression of spiritual dis-ease, which was signalling their transit, together, through their individual dark night of the soul.

The body sweats intensified, irritating Noah's already troublesome skin.

'Are we dying? Do we need to go to the hospital?' Noah chatted away in his head.

As they had just encountered a month long hospital experience this was not the place they had wanted to revisit, unless absolutely necessary (as it had been in order for them to conceive a child). Both concluded that they were likely to only receive an impersonal and standardised level of attention, be placed on a drip, and left to sweat it out in the stark emergency ward. Having taken this under consideration, they decided it best to remain in the comfort of their own home and totally surrender in an act of courage, bravery and complete faith in their body.

When one is under the grip of such viral terror, there's not much on earth at that moment that matters more than one's own wellbeing, and getting better. Noah was in the clutches of mental vulnerability and felt deeply frightened. He was rotting into what he had hoped was not a state of complete breakdown, rather hoping that it be symptomatic of a breakthrough, an everlasting victory. Perhaps this affliction had manifested for Noah as a fitting reflection of his inner world, a mirror to his compiled mental and emotional traumas.

The symptoms kept intensifying. There was a deathly lack of vital energy as the wretched plague inhabiting their bodies, unleashed with supremely destructive power. Neither could fathom the thought of food. It was all they could muster to simply lie there, flat out floundering in a pit of doom.

The clock struck 7:00pm, normally too early to turn in for the night, however, under the circumstances, they were capable of doing little other than nothing at all, so it suited them perfectly. They desperately wanted a break from the heavy experience of the beast, even just for a couple of hours. They drew the curtains and decided to make an attempt to exit the fray.

'Get a good night's sleep sweetheart,' Noah muttered to his wife, who was only inches away drowning in sweat laden sheets and fighting off imminent dehydration. He kissed her on the forehead, slumping back into the pillow.

'You too hunny,' she wearily uttered back.

Noah being a sporadic snorer managed to drift off into the astral realms. For Noah, his *Spiritual Flu* had incubated long enough, it was time for the virus to take its final hold, to inflict the mortal wound on his past, to decompose his present and birth him into a new future.

VII

VALLEY OF THE SHADOW

"Though I walk through the valley of the shadow of death, I will fear no evil, for thou art with me; thy rod and thy staff, they comfort me."

— *Psalm 23:4*

It was late in the night. Noah's compromised body laid sleeping, his consciousness now firmly grasped by the talons of the flu. Aurora woke to make a trip to the bathroom, approaching it slowly, mindful that due to the dizziness she might otherwise risk passing out on the way. Having returned to bed she observed her husband asleep, noticing furious twitching in his hands, tense muscular contraction in his legs and a shallowness in his breath. He appeared unusually disrupted — to where had he travelled in his journey into the quantum, she contemplated.

Noah had plummeted rapidly into the most frightening nightmare of his life, into the heart of the contagion. He had been transited through a very personal portal and thrust into the lower dimensions. These are the realms spoken of by the shamans, depicted in mysticism and revered in folklore. They are the lower and middle worlds, the hidden subterranean underworlds connected to the astral plane, which exist, although unapparent to those on the surface.

His sleeping awareness instantaneously became oddly visual and highly sensory, and this was uncharacteristic for Noah, as he didn't often dream vividly. He'd been catapulted through a profound vortex and dropped in a world otherwise foreign to him.

✳

There he stood, somewhat bewildered, in assessment of the stark and desolate surroundings. There was a lack of illumination, only a misty fog and the faint outline of structures on either side of a road, which he had appraised as buildings. It was as though this scene had been purposed requiring that one feel their way through it with the heart, rather than the faculties of the eyes or thinking mind. Instinctually, he chose to move forward and thus, began to walk. Each step he made was in careful uncertainty, as he nervously surveyed the area for any sign of life — but there wasn't any. The environment projected as like a combination of an abandoned town and that of an old western film set. Visibility was poor and the air carried a morbid heaviness, and for that reason, he felt an unease.

Was this mysterious dreamscape a world of his creation, constructed from the sum total of his pain, sadness, emotional and mental traumas? Or was it the scene of a final drama, the place where he would be compelled to confront his darkness, reveal his demons and release his soul?

Despite the eery stillness prevailing, he gingerly progressed along the road. He sensed quite a contradiction, as there was also the presence of a peace and tranquility interwoven into the otherwise peculiar town.

Noah continued on, intuiting that as the most appropriate course of action. This progress had transported him toward the centre point, the antithesis of the *Spiritual Flu*.

Having increased somewhat in the confidence in his ability to inner guide himself along the way, he momentarily halted, reaching a section of the road that intersected with a vast square, a piazza of sorts. The area was enclosed by a nine foot bluestone wall, and entry into the space was through large timber gates. The gates resembled those indicative of being from the Middle Ages, from the medieval period. They were fixed with thick brass hinges and there was a simple locking mechanism. They were grandiose, likely to have been skillfully crafted from a prolific single piece of aged wood. Noah evaluated the space, deeming it probable to be an arena, or perhaps a place where the residents of the town once met, entertained each other and watched performances. Was it a Romanesque gladiatorial stage, where in a time, those who had been enslaved, faced mortal peril in the name of sport? Was it a representation of purgatory, the principality between life and death, where souls having trespassed against the light encounter review, rehabilitation and reconciliation?

The short period paused in examination of the square motivated Noah to pose pertinent questions as to the rationale of the experience.

'Where am I? What am I doing here?'

Without answers forthcoming, and due to the mist condensed by the surrounding wall, Noah moved to obtain a clearer view of the arena. He glanced beyond the gates.

As in the depictions of mythology, Noah was astounded to observe a prodigious beast, which in his immediate assessment, measured somewhere in the vicinity of twelve feet seated — it was the first sign of life. By virtue of its outline, it beared resemblance to a cat. It sat proudly in the middle of the square, overwhelming the scene. Upon closer investigation, Noah was able to make out faint spotted markings, characterising the animal as that of a jaguar, a *Black Jaguar*. It was beautiful, sleek, thickly set, elegant and powerful, and its coat shimmered with a dark grey hue. Its bright green eyes pierced and threatened, whilst at the same time communicated a subtle overtone of compassion. It was a being of profound potential power, yet it emanated such a signature of peace.

The cat became aware of Noah's presence in its domain. Normally, in life, when one is confronted with the threat and danger inherent in a beast possessing superior power, agility, speed, weaponry and smarts, it invokes the deepest sense of fear for survival, and of potential death. But strangely, as they locked eyes, Noah experienced none of these emotions. Whilst he stood motionless in complete awe of the animals obvious prowess, a peace flowed through him, and any potential threat that he had felt initially, ceased to exist. For Noah there was an unexplainable understanding that this animal meant him no harm, and that rather its presence was symbolic of something transformational.

Often messages of an important nature, originating from the higher domains, are communicated to us through the transmission of signs, often presented in archetypes. It is through the interpretation of these signs, that we are able to understand this guidance, and learn to recognise that this assistance is always available to us.

Noah, with conscious awareness, in this lucid dream state, examined the situation, concluding that seeing the cat, in the otherwise lifeless habitat, was in fact significant.

'Okay, so I've made eye contact with this beautiful creature and I'm not at all frightened...a little apprehensive, but I don't sense any real danger. It's more a feeling that the cat represents something for me, something related to the continuation of my journey down this path — it's as though an unseen force is urging me to keep moving forward. Perhaps it will lead to an exit point, a way out of here...'

Noah, challenged for choice, decided that in the interests of reaching an end, he would be best advised to move on. There appeared no other option but to walk a straight line down the middle of the solitary road that constituted this surreal place. The predominant impetus now was one of prevailing empowerment; the exchange with the impressive animal instigated a transference of power.

Unbeknownst to him, the appearance of the jaguar, as in shamanic belief, had tuned him toward a heightened awareness of his surrounding. For in nature, the jaguar is the master in the wild art and skill of survival. It has ears that can sense the faintest of movements. It boasts a powerful sense of smell and piercing eyes that are able to penetrate through the darkest of nights. The jaguar had shared these qualities, its ability to locate and sense out danger, imparting it onto the man walking the path of the unknown.

Noah sensed danger. Some seventy metres away, stood a solitary small figure. Given the poor visibility afforded by the fog, Noah was surprised that he had been able to see it there so far in the distance. He had as much *felt* the presence, as much as he had seen it — but somehow, he knew what it was. Not withstanding its non-threatening demure stature, its energy triggered an instantaneous and very adverse reaction in Noah. It agitated the memory of something latent in Noah's cells, a memory from a past incarnation — what he saw, he knew to be a *Boggart*.

Popularised in English folklore, Boggarts are devious and mischievous little creatures. In other parts of the world they're known as bogeymen, and are often malevolent spirits who have become attached to a particular location. With a propensity to transform into the worst expression of a person's fear, they carry a serious capacity for evil and like to play games tormenting their prey. They have the ability to shape-shift, changing their form at will, in an effort to trick their prey into trusting them — however, this one had made no attempt to conceal its identity or true nature. It had taken on humanoid form albeit, an ugly manifestation at that. He displayed beastial attributes, bearing over-sized mottled hands covered in gooey sores, bloodshot untrustworthy eyes and an excessive amount body hair.

So unnerving was Noah's interpretation of this nefarious energy, he abruptly, and very sternly, shouted to the boggart.

'Don't even think about it!'

It was a command delivered with the conviction of a person that sensed their life was in danger; and this seriously intended warning to the entity demonstrated that. The creature disappeared immediately, which was uncharacteristic, as they're never shy in coming forward in a confrontation. Noah summated that it had likely cloaked itself and was in the midst of reappearing in another form, and prepared himself for the imminent attack.

Continuing down towards what appeared to be the end of the path, Noah finally reached the junction he had expected to find.

Without warning he was abruptly and violently grabbed, the attacker taking him by the right arm, attempting to pull him closer and attain physical dominance. Noah wrestled with all the energy and strength he could summon, in efforts to keep the dark energy at bay. It felt as though the entity wanted to take his life. The struggle continued in earnest, with Noah aggressively drawing on every inch of his might, to break loose of the vice-like and unrelenting grip the creature had. It was a struggle and he wasn't successful in breaking free. He vainly attempted to kick the dark man away, but as the stand-off was at arm's length, his legs didn't reach its target. Noah attempted kick after kick, but failed in any efforts to release himself.

Whilst still in the clutches of the murderous villain, Noah analysed the situation, concluding that he just needed to wait for the right moment. He decided on a strategy whereby he would trick the dark man, leading him to believe that he had relinquished the fight and succumbed. Noah's plan was to allow the villain to pull him closer, close enough so that the condensed energetic force of a kick, would land and be enough to regain freedom.

The dark man took advantage of the opening and pulled Noah closer, yanking him by the arm that he had fixed onto with surprising seizure. In the instant before the dark entity could inflict a fateful blow, Noah struck harnessing a momentous reserve of elastic energy, collected in readiness for the victorious blow. He executed a prolific donkey kick with both legs, transmitting the prodigious force directly to the Boggart's abdomen. It transferred all the energetic power he could summon in a single expression of kinetic force.

Noah had embodied the stealth attributed to the cat. The jaguar is an intuitive hunter, it knows the best time to strike, seizing the perfect moment for which to take its opportunity, and deliver its lethal blow. Noah had similarly, waited patiently for his moment; he had cleverly lured his attacker into a false sense of security, and then with sheer precision, delivered the forceful blow.

✳

The clock struck 4:44am. Noah had instantaneously woken up, as his body launched rapidly out of the bed, having delivered the knockout blow that ended the struggle. Aurora, disturbed by the sheer force, was woken suddenly, alarmed by the sudden jolt.

'Are you okay? You just launched right out of the bed.'

'I just had the worst nightmare of my life — someone was trying to kill me. It's okay, go back to sleep, I'll tell you more in the morning.'

Despite being shaken and exhausted, Noah decided to get up and attempt some level of normal function. He was not enthused by the idea of staying in bed, in the event of being thrust back into the abyss. He made coffee in an attempt to self-confirm himself into normality. He dismissed his mental inclinations to relive the dream, for if he did, those thoughts only brought back the feelings of terror he had experienced during the ordeal — it was still so fresh in his consciousness.

Nightmares provide us with insight into the content of the sub-conscious and under-conscious mind. They can perform a valuable function in revealing to us where our deepest darkest fears, issues and limitations reside. Manufactured from jumbled, non-related fragments of an individual's consciousness, this debris congeals to form an expressly realistic sleep-state experience. There's often a common thread — sensations of falling, running away, being attacked, of nakedness and the experience of embarrassment. We've all taken these trips into the first and second dimension, meeting with our personal ghosts and interfacing with the entities of the astral realm. Within the nightmare space, the distance between what is real to us, and what isn't, is blurred considerably as we reconcile ourselves and grow through the experience.

As he sipped his coffee, he came to realise that in the moment he discovered the jaguar, he had both everything to be afraid of, and nothing to be afraid of. It was in the transcendence of that paradox, that he was able to continue on confidently walking the path, until which time he came face-to-face with the fight for his spirit, the battle of dark versus light.

This had been the nightmare to trump them all.

VIII

AT THE DAWN OF AWAKENING

"There are no more maps, no more creeds, no more philosophies. From here on in, the directions come straight from the universe. The curriculum is being revealed, millisecond by millisecond; invisibly, spontaneously, lovingly. As one of Thomas Merton's monks has it, 'Go into your cell, and your cell will teach you everything there is to know.' Your cell. Yourself."

— *Akshara Noor*

It was Friday, and the second day of the contagion. Its outward journey denoted the process whereby their physical bodies and auric layers would be purged of accumulated spiritual pain, trauma and dis-ease.

Aurora had slept sporadically. Noah, suffering from fatigue after the nightmare, struggled to resist the temptation to further hypothesise as to exactly what it was that had assumed complete dominion over them.

Mindful of their responsibilities, Aurora proactively rescheduled their shifts with another team member's. She notified their employer of this, advising that both of them were not fit for work. This was met with disdain by the owner.

'You need to provide doctor's evidence.'

The response infuriated Aurora and she tossed the phone onto the bed, voicing expletives before laying down again. She'd hardly moved since returning from taking that morning class the day prior.

'Who was it?' Noah asked, having witnessed the obvious frustration at what she'd just read on the screen.

'It was work…they're demanding we furnish them with a medical certificate! They must seriously think we're both just pretending to be sick!'

Integrity, honesty and trustworthiness were all virtues inherent in the couple and ones they held in esteem as being fundamental, innate and simple. The brash communication had pressed Aurora's buttons; it angered her greatly that their integrity was being directly called into question. The obligations for that day had been covered, so there was no need for the situation to have been dealt with in such a heartless manner — some compassion, empathy and a little understanding was all they would've liked.

Aurora found it difficult to cast off this frustration which continued to grow, compounding the already stressed state of her body. Noah compassionately conveyed his understanding, having concurred with her agitation.

'Don't worry about it babe, let's just deal with it when we're feeling stronger. We don't have the energy to focus on it right now.'

Aurora needed some time to settle, as for her this was a major character assassination coming at a time of great physical and emotional fragility.

Noah decided to shift the topic of discussion.

'I need to tell you about my nightmare!'

'Yes! What happened? You seemed terrified when you woke up!' Aurora replied.

Noah recounted the dream outlining the eery setting, the presence of the black jaguar, and his experience of the dark forces that had threatened him.

'...I was scared for my life, seriously scared — it felt *so* real. That's why I must have kicked and jolted so hard! I'm so glad I didn't hurt you.'

He concluded the abbreviated version of events in order to avoid extrapolating it more than he was willing to. It felt unpleasant to relive because it was still very fresh.

For the entirety of that day the cycle in their household was identical to what it had been. A repetitive routine of sweaty sleep, waves of emotion and persistent visits the bathroom.

One immediate and important concern was that of hydration; the water supplies were running dangerously low. Additionally, there was a shortage of food in the cupboard, particularly of anything plain, in the probable event that they would eventually attempt to eat something.

Noah contacted a friend, a Liverpudlian named Gerrard, who was also living abroad. Given their predicament, Noah asked if he could bring them water and some plain crackers, when convenient. These were the required bare minimums of existence, that which they were physically unable to go and get themselves.

Voluntary acts of kindness are actions born of compassion and empathy, and gifted from one human being to another. In a dystopian world, where human beings have been infected through the promotion and reward of service-to-self behaviours, most are predominantly motivated by consumption, the pursuit of material acquisition and are guilty of energetic vampirism. On the contrary, when one lives in accordance to the principle of service-to-others (the organic human expression), we experience the most reward and feel our best. Thus, those who are naturally giving are those who reflect these innate human attributes — such people are powerful instruments of love.

Gerrard promptly delivered these items accompanied by a kind wish for a swift recovery. He was an intelligent and generous soul, a true friend who took pride of place amongst the small group of people across the globe the couple regarded as kin.

For three days it was to last. First century midrashic tradition held that only after three days, could you be sure someone was dead. Curiously, as its written, Jonah had spent three days and three nights in the belly of the sea monster.

It was Saturday, and the third day of the dire infestation. Both had cried, sweated buckets, had full blown diarrhoea, vomiting, weird lower back pain, itchiness, severe fatigue and thumping sinus headaches.

After two days of not having even the appetite to eat a solitary cracker, Noah instinctively knew there'd be no better remedy than the ancient, tried and tested *'Jewish Penicillin'* — chicken bone broth. He'd cooked it before back in their homeland and discovered it to be an effective solution for treating many an ailment. It would be the perfect antidote to the dehydration and depleted state of their bodies.

Nutritional sustenance supports the survival and the optimum functioning of the physical machine. Chicken soup curiously dates back some seven to ten thousand years and appears to have been utilised for the same very reason, as a panacea for dis-ease! It had acquired a reputation as a folk remedy for colds and flu in many countries. Recent studies indeed supported what the ancients had discovered, and stated an invaluable fact about this concoction; it contained an amino acid, *cysteine*, very similar to the patented pharmaceutical drug, *acetylcysteine*, coincidentally prescribed by doctors to patients with bronchitis and other respiratory infections.

Noah was accustomed to playing the role of both the healer and the designated cook. Despite the reluctance to stand in the kitchen and prepare it (as this seemed energetically implausible), he deemed it a worthwhile sacrifice, such was the elixir's demonstrated benefit.

Noah put out the call for aid.

'Hi Bobby, can we ask a favour of you? Would you mind bringing us the following grocery items; organic carrots, celery, parsley, brown onions, garlic and chicken bones. We are really unwell and would appreciate it so much.'

Fortunately, through recent interactions, Noah had quite synchronously discovered that their friend Bobby resided on a large parcel of land nearby, where he pasture raised chickens and produced organically grown vegetables. Upon hearing of the couple's predicament, the local man of thoughtful disposition, was most accommodating to their needs.

Noah liked to flow and improvise during cooking, slightly altering the traditional recipe to exclude the parsnip. Nevertheless, he felt his permutation preserved the brew's great taste and goodness, whilst respecting traditions.

Noah's now deceased step-father, Joseph, had introduced him to the traditions of the Jewish people and to this soup. It was the recipe of salvation, one that had stood the test of time, and been passed through the generations. Most of all, when you drank of the golden elixir, it made one feel instantaneously better. As Joseph was by lineage, a descendant of the magician, Houdini, Noah had always ratified a magical power about this broth.

A magical artistry also permeated through Joseph's artful hands, not only was he by trade, an extremely talented tailor, having been educated in the ways of couture in Paris, but he also possessed the soothing hands of a healer and regularly relieved Noah's study headaches. Noah loved him dearly as he had become an all-important guardian and mentor for him through a critical period; from the age of eleven through to twenty-two.

Joseph was love in its many expressions and he took Noah under his wing as a son of his own, loving him without distinction to that a 'blood' son (one of which he already had). Born 17th August, Joseph coincidently shared the same birthday as Aurora. This was a curious connection and both shared traits such as perfectionism. Both loved with a generously open heart, delivering the infinite and unconditional love that Noah thrived on.

The man had played a crucial role in his step-son's life, thus Noah suffered immense grief when he passed suddenly in the arms of his mother. Following his tragic death by heart failure, the chicken soup became anchored as a source of remembrance of that love, and the nectar of his spirit.

As the soup simmered away for hours, Noah marveled at the way the soup moved within and of itself. Staring into the pot he could see small particles, like stars, being emitted from the depths of the pot, darting up and out onto the surface. Noah called Aurora over into the kitchen to take a look into the pond of goodness.

'See, look, when you look down into the soup it's like you're flying through the stars, isn't it?' he declared wondrously.

It was but one example of his application to conscious and mindful practices; a determined attempt to reach back into simplicity, hold gratitude and appreciation for even the smallest, seemingly insignificant things in life.

Wonder and observable things of enchantment always surround us, but people too often walk with their chins set down, sadly distracted, utterly detached and therefore missing these opportunities to witness magic.

The rising of the sun the next day brought with it a sense of rejuvenated hope. After the three days in his wretched, sweaty and isolated cell, Noah emerged encompassed by a refreshed attitude, there was a newness around life. These inspirational energies motivated him to compile a list of mandatory life changes in his leather bound notebook. It had been gifted to him by Aurora, affixed with a note; 'Please start writing.'

As he noted:

Sleep —	*Purchase an 'earthing' sheet.*
Air —	*Purchase indoor air purifier (no a/c).*
Water —	*Change filters regularly.*
	Buy reusable blue glass bottles.
Clothes —	*Wear only natural and organic fibres.*
	Hang washing inside to dry.
Move —	*Stretch, strengthen regularly.*
	Play social tennis.
Body —	*Book a chiropractic session,*
	'atlas adjustment'.
Food —	*Cook at home, eat more protein!*
Mind —	*Meditate; clear emotional / mental debris.*
Create —	*Sketch, colour-in.*
Sound —	*Play music, Beethoven.*
	Use healing tones and frequencies.
Technology —	*Purchase more Orgone pyramids to diffuse*
	increasingly harmful EMFs and radiation.
	Unplug WiFi and connect to Ethernet.

Along with the compilation of dot points, Noah devised a schedule for each day outlining what he committed to making routine. Perhaps the most powerful of the words he penned were *'WRITE'* and *'LIVE IN THE NOW MOMENT.'*

IX

RESURRECTION

For the next week, life revolved around replenishment, restoration, copious servings of the chicken soup, intensive rehydration, uninterrupted sleep and the overall revitalisation of their physical bodies.

All their commitments had been fulfilled. Noah had surfaced with energy enough to take up the slack individually, as Aurora had been lagging behind. She had suppressed the full manifestation of the contagion when she had, against her better judgement, chosen to roll her sick body into work on the Thursday. This decision served to prolong both the process of healing, and her subsequent return to health.

The couple operated as a cohesive unit. They complimented each other's relative strengths and weaknesses perfectly, in both the personal and professional context. The couple's relationship redefined the stereotypical gender roles, with Aurora managing the finances and Noah doing the cooking. This automatic ability to find harmony demonstrated just how in sync they were and this amplified the power of their partnership. The experience of being incapacitated at the same time though, had presented unprecedented challenges, and chartered them through unknown territory.

Feeling somewhat rejuvenated, Noah resumed his customary role. He took great joy in nurturing his love, thus concentrated his maternally oriented efforts in expediting Aurora's return to vitality.

Aurora was born of Italian lineage. Food was naturally at the centre of the universe for these families, as it functioned as the glue which unified people.

The traditions of Mediterranean cultures maintained some prominence in their life, chiefly through Aurora's loving relationship with her paternal Grandfather, Dino. He was larger than life, a man whose heart belonged to Opera. He was Italian through and through, the quintessential example of what it is to be from those parts — extraverted, loud and festive! Dino had sadly passed back into the eternal during the fourth year of their travels. His passing had rocked Aurora's world and saddened Noah considerably.

Dino loved Noah dearly and had welcomed him into the family with open arms. He appreciated Noah's interest in his culture, exemplified by Noah's willingness to intently listen to his proud tirades about anything Italian, along with stories about life back in his small hometown.

Noah took great joy in keeping the traditions and the heritage alive, by recreating the flavours of the Tuscan hills. He used food, with the intention of healing — it served as an expression of his deep love for Aurora and also in memory of her Grandfather.

It was lunchtime, and Noah had prepared quite a spread — caprese salad with pesto sauce, focaccia, peppers, olives and homemade pumpkin risotto. The couple enjoyed the diversity of flavours, particularly after the fast that had spanned numerous days.

Feeling well satisfied, Aurora laid down for a siesta on Noah's insistence, whilst he cleaned up the kitchen that was in quite a mess.

With Aurora catching up on much needed sleep, Noah decided that it was an opportune time to undertake quiet investigation into the nature, symbology and mythology of the jaguar. He had only just reached the stage whereby he was willing to recall the details of the dream, and this drove him towards the exploration of the deeper personal meaning.

He drew his own initial conclusions. Given the cat hadn't bared its teeth, nor displayed any aggression toward him, he determined it to be somewhat of a good omen, perhaps even a messenger. He considered that its appearance, quite possibly, represented that of a guardian or protector, to guide him forward on his journey and subvert him from capitulating to the dream. Its function, he wondered, may have been for the purpose of coursing his spirit through the *Flu* state, only to emerge renewed and re-birthed into a re-engineered future; the sort of complete future that he had in futility spent the last decades of his life attempting to cultivate and manifest.

Noah sat himself down at the small desk and opened the laptop in order to commence the research which would help him to reveal the significance of the cat. He purposely hadn't interacted with any of their digital devices since that first morning. Whenever he interfaced with either a handset, or a tablet, he rapidly experienced drain and over-stimulation to his nervous system. Being so unwell had rendered such devices dormant, spending almost a week in aeroplane mode.

Noah had for many years been somewhat dismayed with the whole notion of the wireless, cashless and technocratic nature of the world as it stood. He took pride in maintaining an attitude of rebellion, committing to not fall prey to the orchestrated reliance on modern innovations like 'smart' phones, the internet and wifi, as too had Aurora. He particularly fought with a reluctance to use smartphones with the knowledge that they were the primary mechanism through which people were tracked, traced and targeted with malevolent technologies in complete contravention of their privacy. The world had undergone an accelerated revolution in the advancement of such technologies. Humanity had been introduced to these harmful gifts illegitimately, designed specifically and in gross negligence to prey on human frailties — to consume, to addict, to take further control of the human mind through dream-spelling and high resolution screens.

The couple had taken many steps to minimise the extent to which their immediate environment and bodies were bathed in this electromagnetic soup of unhealthy and discordant frequencies. It concerned them just how much the collective had become the servants to those distractions, at the detriment of their own health.

They had a strong awareness of the dualistic nature of this technology — the fact that it can also be used for good. Without it, the like-minded and heart-based human beings would lack the thread of connection, rendering them to more of an isolated experience of life. But nonetheless, modern technology encouraged distraction, addiction, inflicted physical harm and steered the beams of mind control programming.

Noah, however, decided to put it to good use and investigate the jaguar. Mitigating the potential for harm, he connected the internet via the wall outlet through Ethernet connection. He immediately received an impetus to email a great friend of theirs, Skye, who lived back home in the mountain ranges.

Skye was a highly attuned being who had dedicated much of her life to the pursuit of spiritual expansion and shared an intimate relationship with the animal kingdom. Noah was aware of her vast knowledge of spirit animals, along with her astute ability to interpret and extrapolate the meaning in signs received from the non-physical domains.

Having composed the message to Skye, Noah delved into his own search for meaning. He was quickly directed to information relating to the family of cats, discovering that the jaguar, was also categorised as a panther, given its place in the larger classification of the *Panthera* genus.

Black Jaguars, as inhabitants of the earth, are rare; they make up only 11% of their immediately related species. They are the epitome of controlled strength and will. Thickly muscled, they bear long sharp claws and devastatingly sharp pointed teeth. Their sheer capacity to express power is disguised in their proportionally slender build. Measuring eight feet in length, and growing to a maximum of only one-hundred-and-sixty pounds, they carry the capability to feast on creatures eight times their relative body weight. They are the perfect predator in many ways, and the mightiest of opponents.

One cute and curious tidbit he found was in reference to Bagheera, from the tale of The Jungle Book, who had served as a protector and mentor to the man-cub Mowgli.

Noah chuckled at this and was excited to share it with Aurora, who loved the classics and such tales. Interestingly, Noah also read, that Gandhi once alluded to the panther as being one of his own personal guides during his lifetime here on Earth.

Noah's study readily led him into the subject areas relating to spirit animals. He was interested to read that spirit animals accompany astral travel, carrying with them a guardian energy and an understanding of death. It was a common theme in that they represented the reclaiming of one's inherent power and the ability to know of the dark.

Noah conceded, that most certainly, the animal had accompanied him through the abyss at the very peak of the flu's grip. Having defeated the dark man with that well-planned kick to the abdomen, the cat had witnessed Noah reclaiming his power. It had escorted him through the metaphysical struggle, the test of will where his courage as a spiritual gladiator was tested, with an opportunity to overcome the forces of internal darkness. It is often said, that which does not kill us, makes us stronger. He realised that the creature had taught him that in the darkness, there be nothing to be feared, as after all, he had emerged victorious in the face of great danger.

In the myths of Dionysus, the panther is a symbol of unleashing desires and the awakening of the kundalini forces. The appearance of the panther, in Noah's life, symbolised a prominent shift out of constant oscillation between polarities, and into a new perception of reality more centred in neutrality. In a Dionysic manner, the panther awakened the unconscious urges and abilities that had been closed down. It signalled a distinct time — the eve of his imminent awakening.

Noah was interrupted by the sound of an incoming email. Expecting it would be Skye, he opened the application.

Skye offered her general wisdom and observation relating to the matter of Noah's dream, and the micro cosmic relevance it possibly held in the experience of his present incarnation. She suggested that the appearance of the Panther, in her understanding of spirit animal guides, was profoundly significant, given the creature's power, the long history of reverence and the cat's position in the hierarchy of totems.

She outlined that spirit animals make their timely acquaintance with people in the quantum spaces (in the places such as the one Noah had travelled to and met with his past). Skye intuitively suggested that Noah had experienced the apocalypse of his soul. This she wrote, often signifies the reaching of a crucial intersection where the decays of the past and the sum total of one's experiences seek reconciliation leading to spiritual liberation.

Noah pondered upon what did appear to be a fitting time for the dream to have transpired. He realised that at some point, he had stopped creating, ceased to truly live, and begun the process of dying. The physical degeneration and spiritual fragmentation projected the darkness that had overshadowed his past. These clouds had brought forth greater experiences of loss, pain, sadness and guilt, compounding the fracture, time after time. For the journey of spiritual expansion along the highway of ascension demands one bravely face the inner demons, acknowledge the traumas, tame the negative ego and work studiously to seek release from the dense burdens of the past.

Skye relayed that the spirit animal heralded the beginning of a new chapter, where Noah would likely experience the freedom of sovereignty found through reconnection. In conclusion, it was her directive that he should sit alone, in silence and meditate in order to glean the purist interpretation and meaning for him. She alerted Noah to being ever so cognisant of the fact that knowledge is best accessed without the influence of any intermediaries and interference; the new age movement was deliberately muddied, engineered to confuse and mislead, via hi-jacked, reconstituted and distorted communications emitted from the *False Light Program*. To this end, she highly recommended Noah undertake his own process of interpretation as it would assure the purity of it.

He sat on this guidance and instantaneous confirmations in his own ability flowed freely. Over the years of struggle, he knew that the gestation and manifestation of his new and unified self, was not going to be achieved through external pursuits, but rather through the inward solitudes of stillness, courage, patience, honest self-observation and the commitment to self-mastery.

Noah decided that he would attempt to reconnect with the panther through meditation. He sat in the silence afforded by the quiet of the apartment, and requested that the animal come forth. In his mind's eye he repeated a verse, a verse of his design, in order to call upon the being.

'Oh great panther, the one who may serve my highest and best purpose, please come to me, I seek your knowledge, wisdom and guidance. Speak to me now.'

The verse was repeated seven times (Aurora's favourite number), and he waited patiently for the universal flow of energy to come through — and it came.

'Hello my dear friend.'

Noah heard the words, but like many of us do when we meditate and seek commune with consciousness stationed in the higher realms, he questioned his own ability to connect, and the authenticity of the energy signature. He wondered if the words originating from the voice, were all simply delusions of his intellectual mind, perhaps an inserted frequency of manipulation, or if it was in fact, a pure transmission through the part of him that was divinely tuned like an antenna.

The panther continued.

'Your people know of me. The natives of your lands often refer to me as an animal guide, a spirit animal. I am this to you. I am a guardian for the now and for all of your life as an eternal being. I now walk with you. I will support you, carry you on my back when needed, and bare my teeth, should you deviate, and again risk losing your way. For I am the messenger of your awakening. I manifested for you, and to you in order to see to it, that you would realise the moment of reckoning, the culmination of your endless toil. For the persistence you showed, you have been granted the invaluable gift of seeing. You may call upon my support and guidance at will and my attention shall be yours. I will not leave your side, for you are my angelic child, a gifted one.'

The voice spoke solemnly, with sophistication, grace, elegance and with momentous power. Noah gave thanks to the cat, the mythical manifestation of the infinite, concluding the exchange with a simple question.

'Do you have a name? So that when I seek your presence I may call you by that name.' Noah, poised in silence, and awaited the animals response.

'You may assign me the name of your choosing.'

'Are you male or female?' Noah posed.

'Neither,' the cat swiftly replied.

'I am neither specifically male, nor female, I am unity. I represent the divine balance and the embodiment of both the masculine and the feminine principles.'

'*Kirrah* is the name I shall use to call upon you' Noah advised.

For Noah, the panther announced more than just a coming into his own power. It reflected a reclaiming of that which was lost, and an intimate connection with the great archetypal force behind it. The panther, the black jaguar of the dream, was in fact, the spirit of imminent rebirth.

In the early Jewish commentaries on the scriptures in the Avodah Zarah, Panther is listed as a surname for the family of Joseph. It speaks of how a man was healed in the name of Jesus ben Panther. Through history and largely because of this, the panther has come to signal a time of rebirth after a period of suffering and death on some level. It has come to imply that old and unresolved issues may finally begin to be resolved. It implies that old wounds will finally begin to heal, and with that healing comes a reclaiming of power that was lost at the time of wounding. Any experiences of childhood and beyond that created suffering, causing a loss of innate power and creativity are reawakened, confronted and transmuted in the presence of the beast.

The aspects that held the memories of Noah's past, started to animate in vivid recollections, particularly memories of childhood. He hadn't remembered much of these times, from birth through to seven, perhaps four or five occasions was the extent of his recollection. He had seemingly forgotten that period, storing it away in cellular memory as future treasure to be uncovered.

The recollections were increasing, and it all came flowing back with greater diversity and clarity. Situations, experiences and times he hadn't remembered for forty-four years all came flooding back. All of a sudden he was able to recognise that in the six years he spent alone with his mother, prior to her marrying Joseph, he had actually blossomed. He captained teams, attained high grades and won the district prize for general excellence. Moreover, he understood he'd been blessed with wonderful parents, and grandparents, that loved him dearly.

He recalled times with his paternal grandmother, for the name *Kirrah*, rekindled the memories of a place he had visited many times with her as a young child, post his parents divorce. It was a beach situated on a pristine stretch of coastline that was famous throughout the world. North-east on the vast sunburnt country, the particular spot was renowned as one of the finest places to ride majestic waves. When the mighty ocean's conditions lent themselves to the unique combination of reef and point, there was magic to behold. On these rare days when the planets aligned, the result was a perfectly peeling body of crisp steep water, upon which artistic men of the sea would ride, painting the face of each wave with their finned brushes. Noah loved watching them and remembered how free, light and happy he felt at that time.

For Noah many of the conclusions he had drawn around his early days, and how this period had affected him, were now proving to be false. Any perceived sense of unease or trauma, he figured, was more likely just symptomatic of the fact that he was highly sensitive. He had miscategorised this innate gift with the experience of an incoherent external world; one for which he, as a small boy, had no means of context. These deconstructions were invaluable in Noah's ability to better witness and reconcile his past. It was an ability aligned to the mechanisms of higher sensory perception, now operating in symbiosis with his conscious mind, following the activations of the *Flu*.

Aurora having just taken a shower fumbled her way through her toiletry bag in search for sanitary items. She had been dealt an unwanted blow, menstruation had come just as she'd actually started feeling somewhat better; she had been resting, sleeping well and was on the up. To her dismay, she was now in for at least three days of nagging pelvic discomfort — a stark reminder that her womb remained vacant.

X

THE REALM OF ASCENSION

Noah managed to read four books in four days. The words sparked his imagination once again and his body radiated greater positivity. There was a genuine newness about him, like he'd upgraded a large part of what needed overhauling, of what he had grown tired of, and had often acquiesced to. He was finally experiencing pure, joyful hope for a brighter future.

He had suffered a long and challenging period of decay and the consequent death of his old self. He had exited that highway of burden that had routed his reality for many decades. Propelled upward on a superhighway of heightened awareness, the flames of the light now burned bright, guiding him towards the ultimate state of being. He felt an inspiration blazing within him that had been elusive to locate, yet was so welcomed.

From this elevation, he was now committed to the disciplines required in order to consolidate the recent monumental change. He knew that if he was to establish the shift as one of permanence, it would necessitate consistency in terms of how he applied himself to matters of the mind, body and spirit. It presupposed the dedication to balanced holistic living, requiring one without fail, do things like get out into the forests, sit on the ocean shore, eat clean, master thoughts and emotions along with practicing meditation consistently.

He had previously felt unclear, unclean and disillusioned. The world around him had reflected this, as it had become a mirrored projection of the murky status-quo. Having taken the new resolutions he had penned seriously, Noah had also taken on an inspired commitment to clearing the space in which they were living.

'I'm glad we got sick. It was actually a blessing rather than an affliction,' Noah announced.

Incarnate life by design, and all the possible experiences we bring into reality, certainly delivers on its capacity for the soul to learn, mature, ascend, illuminate and ultimately reach enlightenment. For spiritual growth to transpire, it demands one embrace each and every experience as a divinely orchestrated learning opportunity, without value judgement, of good, bad, right or wrong. Life is thus, precisely purposed to set the existential stage upon which we, as eternal souls, may reveal our higher purpose, complete our individual missions and emanate our soul's highest expression. We must therefore accept, that by design, the fundamental mechanism through which spiritual learning takes place on this planet, is through material world experience.

'I have realised that all I have endured or experienced in my life has made me what I am today, and I'm proud of it. I'm not a victim to my past, I am the victor of my learning.'

In Noah's mind, the virus pleaded to reveal further prophetic meaning. In combination with the dream taking place at the height of the lurgy, it was unlikely that these two elements weren't related. Aurora was likewise intrigued by the likely connection, and encouraged Noah to delve deeper with the inquiries.

Motivated by the potential for insight, he opened the laptop once again, and punched in the array of symptoms that they'd encountered. Dominating the results was a plethora of standardised western medical diagnosis carrying a fear-based signature, with which he didn't resonate at all. Having decided to refine the search, in an effort to avoid receiving another generic stream of results, Noah immediately begun to reveal some compelling evidence in return. It aligned coherently with what their intuition had been telling them all along.

The spiritually oriented information, was suggesting they'd experienced what was defined as ascension symptoms. This set of symptoms, commonly experienced by many, was associated with the procession of the celestial cycles, planetary changes and major shifts in frequency.

'Did you know, most people who experience a spiritual awakening and move into a heightened awareness, also experience something similar to what we just have?' Noah relayed.

'When it occurs, and the relative time it lasts, varies from person to person.'

For Noah and Aurora, it culminated in a shared experience of three days of agony, highlighted by a myriad of symptoms. In divine timing it reached them when they were ready to break free from the chains of the past that had served to spiritually suppress, repress and enslave them.

'It's like it has cleared away the dead wood and propelled us into a future life where we now hold a higher frequency,' Noah continued.

The couple knew that the planet was transiting though an evolutionary cycle of change. These were the times of prophecy, and universal transformation.

'We are a reflection of our Earth, she is changing rapidly, and so too are we inspired to change along with her,' Noah stated.

Aurora sat focused intently on Noah's explanations around the relationship between the earth changes and the ascension symptoms, and the consequential relevance to them. It was evident that there was something meaningful about the entire experience, and her spirit emphatically told her that something dense had shifted.

The traditional Chinese philosophies of medicine in particular, tell us that purging is essential in the detoxification and healthy function of our bodies. What had manifested, to one without context regarding the nature of deep cellular detoxification and its relationship to spiritual activation, would be assumed to be an aggressive virus. But in truth, it was highly likely that the couple had experienced, a rare simultaneous, physical manifestation of something metaphysical in nature — it was, metaphorically speaking, a spiritual flu.

For many, what emerges from such phenomena, shares observable symptomatic similarities with an extreme case of the common cold, but to experience the *Spiritual Flu,* doesn't equate to having had such a thing. It is a transcendental condition that emerges through an infinite array of materialised forms. For some, it presents as a malignant tumour, a suicidal psychosis or a near death experience, for others as a painful loss, an emotional breakdown, depression, or as commonly experienced by star-seed beings, an otherwise unexplainable purge.

The *Spiritual Flu* exists at the macro cosmic level, reflecting and revealing itself through individuated expression on the micro. How it manifests itself outwardly is different, it's divinely personal and appropriate. It's forged by things like soul purpose, life mission, karmic debts, agreements, ancestral and spiritual lineages. To that end, it was possible that the couple had taken on a role as *genetic pathcutters,* prematurely transmuting a code-named consciousness plague.

This *Flu* silently navigates its way through the body and its multi-dimensional layers, scavenging for our garbage, going to wherever needs cleaning, to wherever our pain, trauma, fear and negative belief patterns reside. It spreads throughout the body, the mind and the spirit, preparing your wings to ascend to the heights for which you aspire to reach, re-integrating with source and setting you free as liberated into the future. It requests of you that you stand up, take stock of your past, forgive your trespasses, resentments, regrets, betrayals and release the pain, trauma, fear and destructive habits. Otherwise, you may choose to stagnate, succumb, fall and ultimately perish.

It incubates over lifetimes, bringing itself to a focal point — the death and decay of the old. It is a virus that grows and attains dominance. As it expels outward, following a long period of incubation, it sheds you of the past and fertilises the seeds of the future. It gestates from a higher state of consciousness, and for those able to withstand the onslaught, it brings about a 'life will never be the same' experience of awakening.

The *Spiritual Flu* is thus, a catalyst for spiritual transformation. There is a distinct likelihood that an individual will inevitably reach this tipping point, the juncture of reckoning and reconciliation, in order to evolve spiritually. It is a frequency of change originating from the cosmos, transmuting through the human bio-energetic field. It seeks to purify the cells of the organism in the process of awakening, leading to the bioregenesis associated with biological ascension.

It therefore carries with it a promise, one whereby through the personal journey down the passageway of the *Flu*, one may overcome the spiritual bondage of separation and isolation. The resultant and invaluable gift, lies in the reintegration with the non-physical part of you that awaits reconnection — your spiritual self. A cradle is then formed, into which the inner child may be safely called back, returning your consciousness into a state of unity. This is the emancipation and the level of embodiment where one again feels sustained in their own light, eternally loved, supported, protected and whole. It brings the illuminated and renewed hope for a future destined to be experienced through unconditional love, peace, happiness and abundance. This awakening and expansion then places one on the path to enlightenment.

Now in the remission phase, Noah delighted in the exceptionally positive emotions that were pouring in. He'd put new rituals in place and experienced sensations as though he was being touched by healing frequencies. He vowed to never again be an obstacle to his spiritual development, nor refuse to follow the guidance of his higher self.

'I often stood in my own way and disregarded the guidance I was receiving,' Noah disclosed with welling eyes and an earnest confidence.

'I feel like a new person! I am not the person I was prior to being sick,' Noah once again exclaimed.

It was a joyful declaration, one expressed with significant conviction. He'd at times before felt change, but only subtle change at that — the big one he'd longed for had never come for him, neither at night, nor during the day. This had been a major reconfiguration in the operating system that was central to the expression of his consciousness.

His awakening had taken place and this elevation unified the once fragmented and disconnected aspects, coinciding with the attainment of a dominant position over the demons and the shadows of the past. This needed to be treated as a condition that had gone into remission for all of his days to come.

XI

THE CHARIOT

After rising, as like a phoenix from the ashes, Noah was inspired to get out and see the sights again. Aurora however, remained introspected. He had reconciled that Aurora's dull mood had been exacerbated and prolonged by the monotony of the four walls of the apartment. It had been a lengthy period isolated from the external world, when their life had been placed in a state of quarantine by the *Flu*.

Noah suggested they spend some quality time outdoors together, as he figured it would serve to reinforce to both of them, that life was able to regain some level of normality. They agreed that it would be an opportune time to visit their favourite local market, as they hadn't been there for some time. It was open everyday except for Sundays and had only been operating for just over a year. They loved the atmosphere, it boasted a variety of interesting stalls peddling a treasure trove of local culinary delights, fusion style foods, handmade items and the odd pop-up stall which dubiously came and went, seldom to return.

The intimate, open air style took advantage of the balmy evenings that were commonplace in that area of the tropics. There were relaxed al fresco bars where one could voyeuristically observe the goings on of the market proper. Following a picturesque sunset, the cute little fairy lights spread warmth throughout the market providing ambient lighting to explore the various wares up close. Despite having been there numerous times before, there was always a new vendor, a new delicacy to try and new bargains to be had.

Noah noticed a large wall mural painted by a local street artist, which took pride of place at the very back of the market. It depicted a colourful cat wearing sunglasses, which was quite a synchronicity. It was a reminder of *Kirrah*, the panther of the dream, and of the cats around the area local to their apartment, which had also taken a liking to him.

One new vendor that had caught Aurora's eye was what appeared to be a fortune teller. He sat occupying a usually vacant spot at the very front of the market. On the table was a small sign advertising personal readings at a very reasonable price. Upon closer inspection, Aurora noticed what she assumed to be a deck of tarot cards hidden beneath a handkerchief.

She'd always been fascinated with tools of divination, with runes and other ancient means of connecting with intelligence stationed in the higher planes. Noah was also accustomed to these methods of prophecy, largely through his family who exposed him to subjects of esoteric nature. The old bag of runes they owned was an heirloom that Noah inherited from his grandmother, and Aurora had an aptitude for reading them. Their preference however, was to rely on their own natural intuitive abilities for guidance, as opposed to a reliance on any derived through external means. As such, they both maintained some level of caution around prophets and fortune tellers.

Noah was somewhat bemused by his apparent willingness to entertain the idea of sitting down for a reading; he was familiar with the sublimated distortion inherent in the tarot. Despite this being the case, he trusted in his own discernment, and planned to simply take the messages from the spread that resonated, discarding the rest.

The card reader sat alone, starved of a client for which to read for. Noah, seeing this as synchronous, approached.

'Hello, I'm pleased to meet you,' said the man.

There was a mystique about him, his eyes were of an old soul, deep blue and quite magical. He wore a very prominent ring, a large dark red ruby encased in intricate silver, which caught Noah's eye the moment he sat down. It reminded him of a ring worn by a Hindu priest that had once blessed them. He too, had similarly deep eyes, the kind of intriguing eyes that you don't witness that often.

The man's eyes peered into Noah's with that same level of penetration as had the priests. The fact that the man was wearing an almost identical ring only confirmed to Noah that he'd made the right decision in taking the plunge. The combination of the eyes and the ring, were just too coincidental, and he expected there were messages to come.

Meanwhile, Aurora browsed the aisles. Moving diligently from one stall to another, she hoped to locate a regular stall which offered beautiful handmade accessories intricately woven from natural textiles.

Noah sat directly opposite the reader. The man formally introduced himself and explained that he would read the commonly used spread of eight cards. He posed no question to Noah, something that took Noah by surprise. He simply cleared the energy of the cards and cut the deck into three separate piles, requesting Noah select one.

The cards were beautifully illustrated, weathered and old. Noah had seen many a tired looking deck of cards before. Having met the acquaintance of a few fortune tellers in the long ago past, he recognised it to be a tell-tale sign of a long-time practitioner of the craft. He gathered the man must have been reading for some time, read for many people from all walks of life and refined his skill.

As directed, Noah pointed to one pile from the three arranged on the table, and the reader took the deck back. A card leapt out from amongst the pack now being exquisitely shuffled by the man. The *Chariot* card had jumped onto the table. This was quite a synchronicity considering that astrologically, the sun had just moved into the zodiac sign of Cancer, associated with *The Chariot*.

The man looked into Noah's eyes, with a dreamy demeanour. It was as though he had moved into a more entranced state, ready to channel the powers of foresight.

'I sense that this card holds symbolism for you? Please look closely, there is a message for you, here in this card, represented as your chariot.'

He paused, interrupting his placing of the cards in the spread to elaborate.

'When a card emerges in this way I am always compelled to examine it. This card, *The Chariot*, represents the forward moving energy that is arising within you, and therefore, suggests the beginning of a spiritual journey. It signifies that amidst the many challenges that will invariably be presented to you on your path, you will in fact, overcome these obstacles, providing you retain your focus, maintain your composure and harness the confidence in your abilities.'

He detailed that the journey he interpreted through the card, was one that Noah was more than ready for, and one that would lead him onto greater things.

'I see you moving into the future feeling motivated, ambitious and in control of your own destiny. This card denotes you as the hero, having overcome many of your obstacles through your strength, determination, focus and willpower. I can sense this energy all around you.'

Noah resonated with this, he acknowledged his own persistence. He aligned with the notion that the search for personal satisfaction, achievement and spiritual illumination, was a distinctively heroic path.

'When you set your objectives and channel your inner power; when you apply discipline, fierce commitment and a dedication to achieve your goals, you will succeed. Through all your failures and rejections, you must show courage and never quit. For the warrior always pushes onwards.'

The reader studied the card further. He took multiple glances at his client, before his face lit up.

'I see a great victory for you, but remember that the card also depicts a deeper story behind how you, the victor, reached that point.'

He spoke of it representing Noah as being successful in finding balance between the heart and the mind.

'As depicted, when you harness these opposing forces, reconciling the inner polarities, you will then begin to move them in the same direction and drive your chariot swiftly toward your destination.'

Ultimately, the reader summated, that for Noah, *The Chariot* depicted what it would take for him to reach his goals, making it clear that it was going to be challenging and require steadfast focus. He concluded, that beyond the chariot, flowed a wide river that symbolised Noah's need to stay in the flow with the rhythms of life, whilst at the same time, forging ahead towards the achievement of his dreams.

Noah was lost for words. The rich symbolism extracted by the reader from the single card had so eloquently reflected the nature of the long voyage he had captained, and the potential to reach the oasis, a personal destination of victory.

The man placed the card to one side of the table underneath a finely polished clear quartz crystal, and moved on. He set out the spread just as Noah had seen it before, and proceeded to forecast the next six months.

'You will still live on here, as you have done for a while now, however, there is one place you must visit.'

The man couldn't disclose exactly where it was, only that he believed Noah hadn't been there before, in this lifetime.

'It isn't a place located in this country, but in relative terms you can reach it quite easily, considering you now have your chariot!'

Noah thought of all the places he hadn't seen but wanted to visit on future travels. There were many places the couple wished to visit, from the Maldives to Jerusalem, Jordan and Uluru. It could have been Machu Picchu, the pyramids of Giza, Sedona, or even Iceland. He sat bewildered at the breadth of possibilities, and was now focused on being attentive to any signs forthcoming, that would reveal the relevant place that awaited him.

'You have a very bright future and you love your wife very, very much. Your connection is deep and a very special one at that,' he observed.

'You have already visited the highest temple here on the island, correct?'

In reference to the question, Noah gathered the reader was referring to the main temple on the island, perched high up on a southern hill. It stood proudly as a symbol of Buddhist philosophy and anchored the theosophical foundation of the place.

Noah nodded in confirmation.

'You must visit this temple again, however this time, on your own. You have a message to be received, that is all I am shown.'

The card reader moved slightly to his left and pointed behind him. There in the middle of the fish pond, had grown a lotus flower, a single bright majestic purple flower. Against all odds, from the murky muddy depths of the pond, it had blossomed in a display of beauty.

The reading ended there. Noah was left to ponder an abstract message about a country not yet visited, and an urgency to revisit a place already touched, only months prior.

XII

TREE OF KNOWLEDGE

Aurora had sunk into a depressive state, speaking of life negatively and putting out an energy of wanting to be left alone. She requested her own quiet time and didn't wish to talk. Her moods wavered greatly, with an hour of positivity often followed by two hours of melancholy.

Both had been catapulted through the same complex universe, yet walked different paths once they'd emerged. The commonness they shared through suffering, had also created a temporary bridge between them. This was an unfamiliar space for the couple to find themselves in.

Their love was deep and they shared a spiritual love for each other, one of a divine union. They were social together, there was magic and the overwhelming sense that they were a perfect fit. Since meeting, they had literally spent almost every hour of every day together; they were physically inseparable.

Nonetheless, Noah knew when his lion needed space. Like the grand old polar bears of the arctic, Aurora needed her own period of pseudo hibernation. It was a seldom occurrence that she wasn't her effervescent self and needed a reprieve from the intensity of their otherwise, symbiotic union. It was however, one of these rare times.

Noah knew the very thing that Aurora needed in order to recharge — massage. Aurora loved bodywork. She loved being pampered and valued the remedial outcomes that massage had historically delivered.

Feeling supercharged and super clear, Noah was motivated to do everything he could in an effort to help Aurora regain the level of vitality that he was enjoying.

'Sweetheart, I've booked you in for a 3 hour spa treatment at Koom's Traditional Wellness Centre.'

She deserved it. Not only had she made her way through the peak of the contagion, she had also endured the consequential interruption of menstruation. Additionally, she had only a fortnight prior, miscarried the baby both of them had for millennia sought to create.

An appointment was fortunately available in enough time to make the trip down south. Noah drove, so Aurora could just lay back, put her feet up and enjoy being chauffeured. He planned to drop her at the spa, then continue down to the very southern tip of the island to sit on the beach. It was only a short way down the main road from the spa centre.

It was a beautiful morning on the island and the traffic had passed through its peak hour. The drive posed no obstacle or fuss, a leisurely thirty minutes was all the time it would take to get there. After ten minutes had elapsed, Aurora having spent the journey in contemplatory silence, sternly proclaimed.

'STOP!!! STOP THE CAR! Pull over...NOW!'

She shouted — the same thing again, and again.

'Okay, I'm trying to get over to the roadside and stop, what's going on?' Noah not having any clue at all as to what the urgency was.

'There's a SNAKE! On the car, on the windscreen, see?'

And there was. The snake must have taken refuge in the engine bay, grown weary of the heat and noise from the running motor, and made for a swift escape. It had been making its way from left to right across the windshield and over onto the wiper arms at the bottom of the glass. It was a bright green snake, of about two metres in length, the thin and long type. Its luminescence was heightened by the rays of the sun and it burst with metallic colour.

'OH! Okay! Hold on! There's motorbikes all round me.'

Aurora pleaded him to just stop. Noah managed to move across the two lanes, safely stopping out the front of a local hardware store. Aurora leapt out of the car, thinking that the snake may find its way inside the cabin. At the same time Noah had decided that he wasn't moving, for surely he thought, the snake couldn't fit through any of the gaps in the exterior of the car. He summated that the most prudent course of action was to stay inside. After all, it had moved from the passenger side of the windscreen, across and to the right, directly in front of him. Being so close to the door on his side, he had decided that the serpent was now too close to risk opening the door.

'Help. Please. Please, help us! Snake, snake…,' Aurora yelled out. She was desperately wanting to attract attention and recruit some help.

The shop owner, an older local man, who was luckily outside assisting a customer, turned, assessed the situation and proceeded to fetch a long metal rod with which to relieve the couple of their unwanted guest.

The emerald snake curled up in its splendiferous hue around the rod and was carried off into the vacant lot — all within alarmed earshot of those intently watching its movement, hoping that its new course be the opposite direction to where they were observing it from. With some confused re-directions the serpent made for the nearby foliage and was gone.

Aurora had quite an aversion to snakes. They're rare for most people to encounter in the course of their days, and she had only once seen one, from a distance. She vowed she would never hold one or even touch one — for Aurora they were in the league of spiders and cockroaches. Noah on the other hand, despite not being fond of them per se, had felt quite at ease with the situation. Perhaps it was due to the fact that he had no other choice but to keep calm, considering he was in control of the vehicle. Besides, he hadn't noticed it until it emerged from the wiper arms.

Once they returned to the road, Noah relayed that he had felt an uncanny peace with the entire event.

'I immediately thought of one word — *transformation*,' Noah conveyed with an assurance.

'I just thought STOP the car and get out! I could imagine it making its way in, I've heard of that happening before!' Aurora in offering up her observation of it.

Upon arriving at the spa, just on time, the pair sat down, sipped on the complementary tea and chuckled over what had just transpired.

There was a sense of disbelief. Both were increasingly experiencing life as a procession of signs and symbols. The event had thus alerted their curiosities to deeper meaning. It all fitted with the now flowing wave of meaningful experiences in their days. It culminated in events that synchronously communicated through universal intelligence. Aurora loved synchronicities and noticed them all the time. They had flowed fast and furiously, to the point that it wasn't surprising any more. It is the way it works, for those with the eyes to see.

Aurora filled out the new client questionnaire, the therapist reviewed it, asked a couple of questions and motioned for Aurora to follow. A hug and kiss were exchanged and off she went.

'See you in a few hours,' Noah waved, as he walked back towards the car.

Noah had solidified his acquaintance with the big cat featured in the dream. On some level he had now also connected with the new slithering visitor. There was a distinctly mysterious and cryptic energy conveyed through the snake's emergence.

He gave some thought to the passage it had taken, and whether its transit provided any insight. It had moved across, left to right, stopped in front of him and looked in his direction (so he was told by Aurora, who recalled every detail). Noah perceived that the snake's particular interest in him, and not so much in Aurora, was an important clue as to what was transpiring in the evolution of his life. It was possible that, in these otherwise inconsequential details, there was information to be gleaned. Potentially, the left to right route it had taken, could be viewed as a linear representation of Noah moving from the past, and facing his future head on.

As Noah made his way down the picturesque winding road toward the beach, his highly inquisitive disposition was already connecting the dots. There was a clear message to be uncovered, one he interpreted as carrying relevant meaning, specific to him.

He immediately drew a connection with the condition of his skin. He displayed the scaled skin, resemblant of the snake. It had been scaly for a long time, it wouldn't readily peel off and was too deep to exfoliate. He resigned to staying out of the sun, as that only made it drier and look significantly worse. It had deteriorated over the past months and was becoming a source of irritation; it was most disconcerting. The crackled dryness, which had taken chronically unpleasant residence over his lower limbs, provided another important clue as to the mystical nature of recent experiences, and that of a higher meaning.

Noah was relatively familiar with the many metaphysical and mythological interpretations surrounding the snake; the most prominent being that the snake sheds its skin in the process of rebirth. The word *transformation,* from that initial intuitive feeling, now seemed fitting. The decayed skin representative of Noah's old self had been shed, revealing a purified, renewed and rebirthed self that had transcended the past. Noah knew that in seeing the snake, it had provided him with tangible confirmation that his personal transformation had likewise, taken place. It signified the time in his life when the process of enlightenment had begun, after the unveiling and the awakening of self.

Not withstanding these cursory observations, the historical use of snake symbology had in fact, played a primary role in the nefarious manipulation of the planetary grids, and in the continued repression of collective human consciousness. The Caduceus geometry, for instance, is an inorganic structure installed into the planetary architecture and used to establish, what is known as, the *Caduceus Network*.

Additionally, at the level of the individual, a metaphysical hitchhiker, referred to as the *false kundalini snake,* had been superimposed upon the human hologram. This artificial implant was engineered specifically to siphon precious life force, *kundalini*, from a person without their knowledge or consent; then utilised to power up a network of alien machinery. The design and purpose inherent in this alien machinery mirrors the state of human reality, as likewise, the perpetrators project and then promote this consumptive modelling on the surface, through service-to-self behaviours.

For Noah, what had transpired through the expulsion of the *Flu*, had effected the removal of this *false kundalini snake*. The snake's appearance on the outside of his 'vehicle', had in fact manifested, so as to represent the removal of this etheric weapon from his vertical channel. He had been released from the constrictive binds that had robbed him of full access to his own creative energies, and long consumed that which was rightfully his; that with which he would now be able to fully draw upon, and flower into his soul's best expression.

In the narratives of the new age, the snake is depicted as *kundalini*, however this relationship has been a purposeful misrepresentation. *Kundalini* by definition, and as a direct translation from Sanskrit, means coiled or spiral. The affiliation of *kundalini*, with the snake, is simplistically based on the similarities shared between the coiled nature of organic *kundalini* energy, and the mere fact that a snake coils when it sleeps. The presentation of this symbolic association is more so, representative of the *Caduceus* system of harvesting. As such, to suggest that *kundalini* and the snake are representative of one and the same thing, is a gross misappropriation. For in truth, *kundalini* is a divine feminine energy laying dormant in spiral form, at the base of the spine.

With Noah alleviated of the *false kundalini snake*, and the drain upon his consciousness, it marked a prominent and transformational shift. It signified the reclamation of his own personal power as a sovereign being.

Noah reached the small inlet. He loved this particular little beach, it was quiet and unspoiled. If one could describe the most perfect setting for collecting one's thoughts, finding tranquility and connecting back to Mother Earth, this would be it. It was a charming beach caressed by a soft breeze, with warm shallow waters featuring rocky grottos that attracted a treasure trove of fascinating marine life. Secluded and sheltered from the elements, the sands backdrop was formed by a line of grand old coconut palms. These palms taking up residence on the beach after having been placed there by the hands of the crystal blue waters. There were two rustic beach swings, shells of all shapes and sizes, and scatterings of fascinating driftwood pieces. All these unique and quaint attributes, made it Noah and Aurora's preferred bathing spot. There was a little shady nook at the end of the beach that they'd discovered on previous visits. Thankfully, that spot had always been unoccupied and this day proved to be no different.

Noah systematically unravelled the beach rug, a locally dyed and hand-stitched Mandala throw, carefully placing it down on the sand. He set out his current book of study, water bottle, the leather notebook and a pen.

He'd frequently looked far out to sea beyond the horizon in assessment of his life. In fact, he had visited this beach many times before the endurance of intensive care in private isolation. He recalled those times, when the greatest disparity existed. His capacity to enjoy the beauty of nature was limited by his somewhat fractured state of being.

This time however, was different, very different. He could feel the heartbeat of his consciousness in perfect symphonic alignment. He had been relieved of the chronic gut butterflies and the stupendously looping thought processes. He had left the discordant aspects of himself, his suitcase of traumas and his karma back there in the nightmare town. What he brought back was a loyal and strapping guardian, a new perspective, an ease with life and a pure connection to a higher frequency of experience.

Aurora, only a short drive back down the main arterial road that split the island in half, was half way through her treatment. She had enjoyed steam and a luxurious exfoliation of her entire body; she too, had dead layers to be scrubbed.

Her mind longed for a reprieve, just as much as her body needed the physical therapy. Finding calm, letting go and reconciling the dualities of her mind into stillness wasn't her forte. But, to her credit as a true student of life, she had been working on it nonetheless.

She attempted to silence her ever-active subconscious voice by concentrating her focus on the disciplines of singular awareness — the breath. She accepted any thoughts, acknowledged them, released them, then synched back into rhythmic breath, with the only sound being the tones of deep abdominal inhalation and cleansing exhalation.

This had been her trustworthy method in finding respite and solitude in these moments; moments when it was difficult to silence insignificant material world concerns and slow chaotic mental activity. For it seemed utterly counter-productive to lay there, supposedly in the space of ultimate relaxation, the spa, whilst the mind rushed from one topic to another, chattering away in mental dominance.

The two therapists (Noah had booked the signature four-hand massage) guided their expert hands around her body in fluid, warm healing strokes, up and then down, each pass adding to the relative comfort of the next. It made for a symphony of subtlety, the movements soothing and the pressure remedial. She managed to settle the voices in her head consumed with mundane topics and proceeded to wander off into a theta state.

Her imaginative mind stirred, capturing an image. She sculpted a beautiful scene and entertained it with glorious innocence. She recalled what it felt like to have her husband's warm hands lovingly caress her body — she melted at the touch of his hand, and had done ever since they met.

It had been almost two months of celibacy, some fifty-six days since she had enjoyed the euphoria and heavenly sensations of their ancient union. She enjoyed the private interludes, which harmonised their aspects into oneness. Her body had been starved of these moments, and her spirit yearned for time in her divine partner's embrace. For Aurora, this drought had been culminating into a longing to unify with her masculine counterpart — she longed for both the spiritual, and the sensory connection.

XIII

EMBODYING THE LIGHT

As though he'd been given new eyes through which to see the world, Noah sat in silent monologue on the small stretch of sand.

'I have changed, I know I have this time, I am now able to live my full truth, to fulfil the destiny of my choosing and live my dreams. I no longer languish as a victim of my life, but rather live as an integrated warrior of the light, embodying the strength, the will and the capacity to triumph. I understand that all things that have come before, only served to cultivate the person I am today.'

As a byproduct of the *Spiritual Flu's* exodus, he had experienced an awakening, which catalysed the reclamation of his precious life force energy. This activation directly translated into an inspiration to embrace his dormant creative talents. The clarity that had emerged as a result of the alignment between Noah's spiritual and physical aspects, had illuminated him with purpose — the darkness had been dispelled and he was now immersed in the ascending spiral light.

Recent indulgences of the intellect, by virtue of the words and concepts in books, solidified a vision of creating his own magic with words — by *writing*. The impressive achievements of his son, further fortified this idea and gave it likely material potential.

For writing was a talent many encouraged him to pursue, none more so than Aurora. She was regularly moved in the reading of his beautifully constructed messages for her in greeting cards, and his meticulous drafting of their wedding vows had been a labour of love. She believed in his pure heart and in his extraordinary ability to connect through the written word. It was the very reason why she had purchased the leather notebook as a gift for his birthday, expressing a wish for him to write, and share his glorious mind with the world.

That same notebook now sat there vacant, begging to be given life. Its blank pages relishing the potential for its owner to give it purpose — to bring words to life.

Noah sat immersed in reverent appreciation for the vast and limitless ocean. He had finally let go of the near-sightedness, and replaced it with a macro lens. As though he had been equipped with the reach of the mightiest telescopes, he now possessed the enhanced clarity that perceived the world differently. He understood that out beyond the horizon, laid an oasis of infinite potential.

Noah was now in a coherent space whereby he was capable of creating his reality, through daring to reach beyond the limits of what he once believed was possible. With this new comprehension he reflected, and cast his future out into the distance. He aimed beyond the point at which the sky met the seas, deciding it was there that he would set forth an intention for the realisation of a dream. He focused his attention on creating what he wholeheartedly believed could be drawn in from over the horizon and brought into manifestation, so as to become real.

As though driven by the most powerful forces in the cosmos Noah decided to commit to ink, a conscious intention, what some would call a 'dream,' to be brought into fruition.

The note reading as follows:

"By the time of my birthday in the year 2023, I will be a renowned author. My books will inspire people all over the world."

He recited the affirmative verse seven times (Aurora's favourite number), lit the note and with ultimate belief, watched it burn. The blackened parchment sunk into the sandy hole ablaze with alchemic power, until it shrivelled into nothingness. It was done — the purposeful intention had been committed to the aether.

Tears flowed from his emotional centre; his solar plexus stirred and released in relief. He had finally discovered the combination to unlocking an ancient and buried treasure. Contained within what had been preserved in time, were the coordinates to a divine and personal purpose. He had now secured the map that would charter his course onward, into a grander mission of pure expression and experience.

It had started to get hotter and the sun was directly above where Noah sat. As his skin hadn't seen much sunlight for some time, it became too oppressive to continue to sit. Checking the time, Noah realised that Aurora would have only been halfway through her treatment. He gathered he'd have ample time to visit the temple (the one the card reader had told him to revisit), as it was conveniently situated back in the direction of the spa. He felt a strong impetus to move with the momentum, get back in the car and go.

Sometime back up the main road, the temple in all its majesty grew nearer. Finding a parking spot and locking up, he took some long, deep breaths in order to reset. Noah had encountered many emotions at the beach and still had slightly bloodshot eyes. The affirmation ritual had unleashed a tsunami of emotions, all positive, with a feeling of release and victory.

As the temple always attracted a plethora of tourist groups, he felt a little vulnerable and unsure. He knew nothing of what he was to find and knew nothing of what he ought do. However, as he'd become more accustomed to doing, he decided that he would simply let himself be guided within the flow, trusting that whatever it was that he needed to see, hear or experience would present itself.

He wandered toward the entrance, past the vendor stalls and noticed a room which housed nine gold Buddhas — a Buddhist place of respect and offering. In synchronous flow with the day, he decided to enquire with the monk manning the desk, as to how one would participate in performing their own personal offering.

The monk passed Noah fifteen incense sticks, requesting Noah light them using the prayer candle that burned on the table. He also advised him not to blow on the end of it once ignited, but rather to allow the incense to find its own way to its smoking point, allowing it to take its natural course. This was accepted with curiosity, as Noah had never heard of this before. He had always blown out the flame on the end of the stick after lighting it. He appreciated this new mindful way of working with the aromatics he often used at home to dispel odours and bathe their space in sweetness.

Additionally, the monk selected one of the posies of marigolds and handed them to Noah. He then took Noah's hand guiding him toward the statues.

'Start with this one, this one first,' the monk clearly relayed.

Each of the five Buddhas, gold ones, received a bow, head to hands and three sticks each. Once all five had been completed, the monk gave the following instructions;

'Look in there' pointing to Noah's heart, '...and ask to be guided to the Buddha who possesses the wisdom you have come to receive.'

Noah put any rational considerations aside and allowed himself to be guided intuitively. He resonated with a tall Buddha whose head was adorned by a number of intertwined serpents. Noah hadn't noticed this feature until the last moment, but it rekindled memories of the snake on the car, another coincidence that was of no coincidence. It linked up in a perfectly harmonious way. The signs were dynamically flowing, the synchronicities were plainly obvious and this was a tremendous motivation for him to remain in that flow, to ride its wave and not fall off. He observed that perhaps for the first time in his life he was truly living present in the moment. Led by trust, faith and a feeling of synergistic connection to the divine.

The monk, seemingly respected Noah's willingness to freely display his emotional fragility, outstretched his hand, and asked if he'd like to accompany him into the main temple.

Upon reaching it, Noah noticed a stall which stocked ornamental Buddhas, trinkets of all sizes, polished marble tiles and blank copper hearts on strings. The tiles could be purchased and then personalised by the buyer with a felt tip permanent marker. The personal message written on the backside of the tile, would then be fixed to the temple exterior as part of the buildings rejuvenation process. With that, one had the unique opportunity to take their place on the temple for all eternity.

As Noah had already participated in this offering on their first visit to the temple, he decided this time to enquire about securing a copper heart of his own. Thousands of locals and foreigners had decorated these hearts with messages of hope, love and prayer, hanging them in the trees that surrounded the temple building.

Immediately, Noah determined that the commitment to his dream that he had just made on the beach, would make the perfect message to inscribe on the blank heart. It would consolidate destiny.

Ablaze in excitement Noah carefully penned his affirmation. He dated it, signed it and set motion for a westerly point on the hillside. He passed many, many hundreds, thousands of messages, each hanging from a small tree, all bunched together in glistening lots. He made towards what he thought was a less cluttered section that presented available space.

Upon the edge of the hillside stood a beguiling tree. It had grown in stark contrast to the other trees as it had developed upward by twisting on itself, separating into two trunks that wrapped and rose. Noah was convinced that this was the tree that should be adorned with his message, as twisted trees often indicate the presence of an energy vortex. Such trees are found in places of significance, places like Sedona, Bali and Tibet.

Not one single brass heart had, as yet, taken its place on the tree. This was the spot. Head to hands, Noah bowed to the spindling tree. He mentally recited his ode to the future and hung the heart under the early afternoon sun. He emanated with delight and reflected the stunning brilliance of the coppery piece. It now swayed proudly in the wind, high on the mount, sending its message out across the ocean in patient wait for the universal law of cause and effect to take action.

The monk who had taken a liking to Noah, had observed the visitors diligent selection of the tree and his careful placement of the message upon a strong, highly set branch; he nodded in respect of this mindful care. He rarely interacted with a visitor to this extent, as manning the booth was his primary task during the daytime hours.

'Come,' the monk said, waving his hand. He directed Noah toward the main temple room.

The sacredness of the place and the possibility of seeing what was inside excited Noah. He grappled with the appropriateness of displaying any excitement in such a place of peace, stillness and quiet, as he felt an overwhelming sense of jubilation. He walked side by side, guided by the monk before finally reaching the entrance.

The room expanded upwards and outwards. It was grand, gleaming and serene. A giant sized Buddha glowed peacefully at the rear, centred to the rest of the room. There at the foot of the Buddha sat a wise and well-weathered Bhikkhu; his demeanour soft, his posture perfect and his body coursing love. The young monk that had befriended Noah, lifted his hand motioning toward the senior monk, perched at the foot of the statue.

'He would like to share a moment with you.'

Noah felt ecstatic to have been invited to meet the Bhikkhu and hoped that they would perhaps share a prayer. Perhaps he might experience a blessing, or connect with the uncommon level of contentment that radiates from the enlightened. Sitting on the floor crossed legged, facing the Bhikkhu, Noah sat up perfectly straight, head over heart and heart over sacral, with his head slightly bowed, just enough to still see the elder's face.

'Breathe' was the only word uttered by the Bhikkhu. They held eye contact in exploration of one another's being. His eyes smiled into Noah's. Noah smiled back with gratitude, and in silent recognition of something that is difficult to express in words. After some three minutes in silent meditation, the Bhikkhu spoke.

'Welcome home my child. Always remember that in a spiritual life you are always at the beginning.'

The Bhikkhu proceeded to hand Noah a lotus flower.

'This is a symbol of purity, a holy plant that is used only for the highest of spiritual purposes.'

He then directed Noah to place the lotus in front of the grand statue of Buddha, as a prayer for his enlightenment.

Noah smiled at the synchronous manifestation of the lotus, in line with what had been alluded to by the card reader. It didn't matter why he had been directed back here, as the profoundness of his experience simply affirmed that he was in tune, that he was being led by forces that dictated that everything fitted into place and was meaningful.

He proceeded to make the offering as per the Bhikkhu's instruction, meditating alone for some fifteen minutes.

Traditionally, if one felt like they had offended God through mistreatment of themselves, others or nature, they would offer a lotus as a form of acknowledgment to the higher self, in asking for the forgiveness of their behaviour.

Within the Buddhist philosophies it is suggested that all people are capable of achieving spiritual enlightenment. For the lotus is a sacred flower symbolising purity, self-regeneration and rebirth. Unlike any other flower on Earth, when the lotus begins to sprout, it is underwater surrounded by mud. Despite these harsh conditions, the lotus doesn't allow the dirt that encompasses it to adversely affect its growth or potential beauty. Even when rooted in a dirty pond, veiled from the sun's rays, it rises above the surface and blooms into the most opulent form, as an example of sheer beauty.

In this sense, the journey of a lotus flower mirrored that of Noah's spiritual journey. The appearance of the lotus on his path, closely reflected much of what he had faced, endured, reconciled and overcome. He had been born into a world shrouding him in darkness, yet whilst encumbered by these repressive conditions, he continued his push upward toward the light, neither diminished, nor discouraged in his quest to flower into the expression of his own innate beauty.

Having lost complete track (or awareness more so) of time, Noah arrived five minutes late for his now refreshed and rejuvenated Goddess. She sat, hair still a little disheveled, quietly sipping on herbal tea in the lobby area.

'Hi beautiful!'

Aurora heard his voice. She turned and rose, arms outstretched awaiting the embrace of her man.

Noah whispered into her ear.

'I missed you, let's go home. I want to feel your body close to mine, it's been so long.'

'Yes, me too.' Aurora coyly replied, as they made their way back to the car holding hands.

XIV

SACRED UNION

When you love someone deeply they become part of you, as like an extension of your soul. For love is the meaning of life. It is infinite in nature, fundamentally residing at the zero-point of creation. It hath no boundaries, no end and is an unrestricted force.

A comfortable warmth in the air presided. They set the mood with soft lighting, and the curtains drawn. Aurora lit three candles, which emitted living light, at both the bedside and on the dresser. Along with the scent of essential oils and the soft blissful sounds of the harp, their bedroom was immersed in tranquility.

Noah and Aurora had always immensely enjoyed each other physically from the moment they met. Love making however, was a celebration of the spirit, not just an exclusively physical experience of the flesh. On these seldom occasions, when time had passed and the couple hadn't indulged their passions for one another, it was inevitable that one would say to the other, *'I miss you'* — and that was all the reminder they needed to reignite the flames of intimacy. There had always been a spirit of innocence and a unique magic. Their fires ignited the deepest passions they held for one another. It had always been that way. They were in love and passionately attracted; physical connection only exemplified this.

The lovers stood facing each other in the trust, honesty and willingness to be spiritually stripped. In complete innocence, only feet away from each other, they were released from the coverage of any clothing, prepared to fully allow the other to see deep inside. They held hands, and became lost in the discovery of each other's eyes. This attentive focus granted a high level of access into each other's being, exposing vulnerability, and dissolving any separation.

The intention was to unite in breath as one, flowing together in the sanctity and sacredness of their partnership. They were bridging their consciousness into a unified field, one loving energy body representing the pure emanation of the profound love that may be shared between man and woman.

They drew closer and met in embrace. Her large, natural breasts pressed up against his athletic upper body, as his pelvis pressed against her. His warm, loving and adoring hands, so purposefully explored her body, making their way in circular motions from the lower parts of her stomach, slowly upwards towards her plunging and exposed chest.

She could smell his signature masculinity, his recognisable scent, and she could hear his breath deepen as his arousal grew simply at the mere touch of her figure. It was a sensory deluge that was invigorating, tantalising and one of pure anticipation.

He chivalrously took her by the hand, inviting her to sit with him on the bed. The spiralling energies catapulted upward, as both sat fully present in synchronised breath, continuing to gaze into each other's eyes.

He began to softly and sensually kiss the nape of her neck, something she had always loved. She momentarily lost the sequence of breath, as her arousal levels escalated from the sensual pressure of his lips.

He caressed her, pressed up on her naked body, his hands moving expertly and lovingly around her every curve. She felt the warmth of his palm encase her entire breast, first one, then two. The pulsing and clasping action catapulted her into a state of pure sensory bliss — she wanted to be taken then and there, to be the fruit of his desire, of his want for feminine and divine connection. This burgeoning craving challenged her inner will, amidst the stratospheric levels of desire.

As the moments passed, both grew in anticipation knowing the physical aspect of their union was drawing closer. The most sacred part of her body had already become eager for more, and she was bursting with swelling urges. Shivers ran up her spine, and stronger contractions flowed within her. She needed to feel his body meet hers, all of it, and to envelop her beloved in prolific bliss.

The pressure to resist each other became almost unbearable, both were feeling the urge to consummate what they had waited so long for. They repositioned themselves, and she guided him inside her, immediately vocalising in satisfaction. As they met as one, they began to move in a harmonious melody of delight. They rocked back and forth gliding with gentle purposeful movement, their pelvis' moving away, then back together. Each plunging thrust fully engulfed her, bonding the lovers in a sequence of deep connection.

With sweat dripping from his brow, his chest and stomach glistened from the intensity of his efforts. She gasped in orchestral release as he penetrated deeply and fully from the powerful drive of his hips — again, and again. She whimpered in pure joy, as he struggled to resist the expulsion of the energy which was set to liberate in a momentous release.

Neither had any awareness of time or place any longer; they had been transported into a different realm, gliding through the dimensions of pure angelic divine love. They were awash in the sacred waters where the potential for creation exists and glorious life begins; on the verge of that imminent moment of culmination. It was sublime physical association fostering an ever greater shared spiritual connection.

They had reached the crescendo of their euphoria, the point of deliverance when their love would flower. Aurora let go and released in cosmic ecstasy, instantaneously feeling the flow of his universe course through her. The waters gushed from within and she dusted her lover's tree of life with her most sacred offerings.

It was at that moment, that the light appeared. It sourced from within them and it surrounded them, bathing them in rays they could feel and see. The couple had reached completion.

Unified as one, bonded from two, their flames had emerged as the loving light of singularity. They had soared above the heavens and the earth had duly moved. For that was only apt, as they had moved heaven and earth, simply to be together in the first place.

XV

SPACE FOR ASCENSION

Recent accelerations in energy, saw the couple endeavouring to close loops, summarise learnings and formulate revised perspectives. They were composing renewed visions for themselves, and their life, with a view to stabilising in the higher frequency.

The *Flu*, during its incubation stage, and subsequent emergence into physical reality, had called upon them to consider their very existence. Both had observed their own steep trajectories and individual growth curves, discovering much on the path that is awakening, and witnessing first hand that, 'when the student is ready, the teacher appears.' The old adage of 'seek and you shall find,' had also proven to be verifiably true.

The transit through the remission period of the *Flu* commanded they continue to navigate the many new frontiers that opened up. It demanded they actively exercise sovereignty in all aspects of life. For humankind was amidst an energetic shift, characteristic of an ascension cycle. This was to be a personal journey of initiation through the process of bioregenesis; a biological ascension, divinely designed for one to integrate the higher aspects into physicality, and thereby actualise their full spiritual potential.

In order to achieve this spiritualised embodiment, we must, with resolute devotion, apply ourselves in each now moment. We must commit, with dedicated attention and self-responsibility, to fostering an optimal environment within, and without. We require healing through clearing, cleansing, nourishment and spiritually mature practices. For this phase, on an evolutionary level, calls upon each individual to put their consciousness in action, and vehemently focus on the attainment of a harmonised state of being.

As such, more so than ever before, Noah and Aurora were compelled to attend to both their spiritual and physical needs, in an effort to heal the damage that had been done to their multi-dimensional health.

Preventative medicine took on an entirely new context in their life. Their steadfast focus was upon the health of each aspect within their trinity of being; the mind, body and spirit — the spiritual house. They vowed to maintain consistent daily practices of meditation and conscious movement, teaming this up with nutrient dense foods.

Nutrition had become a major body of work for Aurora. Her study of agricultural practices, ancient nutrition and the essential needs of the human being, had entailed many hours of investigation. The learnings gleaned were of paramount importance in relation to their goal of achieving total holistic health, and maintaining it.

The aspirational search for meaning and truth, within the deep exploration of everything, is a mindful practice. It requires one bravely question, compare, overlay, analyse and maturely discern all that they interact with. The discovery of true knowledge takes time, effort and dedication, as too does the integration of that knowledge. Thus, the process of waking from the dreamspell, and moving back into one's own luminosity, can be an utterly frustrating undertaking.

The accepted narrative of the mainstream has falsified many facts, across many topics, constructing an infinitely deep and elaborate web of lies. It is a complex and multi-dimensional system of inversion, control, repression, suppression and harm. For humanity has faced a diversity of historical threats, including damage to the planetary architecture, the geo-engineering of the biosphere, the manipulation of weather and the seeding of nano-tech. The soil we walk upon has been tainted beyond comprehension, there has been genetic modification of our food and poisoning of the water we drink. People have become addicted to opiates through an orchestrated system of sickness, profiteered by the *pharm*aceutical industry. Our minds and behaviours have been socially engineered through the education system and the silent sounds of mass mind control. Finally, but not exhaustively, our bodies at the cellular level, have been exposed to unsafe levels of electromagnetic radiation through the use of wireless and 'smart' technology; for we are living in times of dangerous technological acceleration and this has placed our bodies under the highest level of invasion. The issues faced by humanity are so diverse, widespread, ingrained, embedded and overlaid. What has been coordinated, by virtue of the over-arching strategies of those in power, is a planetary sickness producing a death culture.

A legitimate mistrust develops during the steep descent down the 'rabbit hole.' Once one sets course into this uncharted territory, there is no retreat, and no going back, as much as at times the activations, the integrations and the birthing pains are immense. The system is cleverly designed to send those who set sail in search of the truth, round and round in circles. It is fraught with danger, traps, lures, trickery, distortion and misinformation — for the treasures of the truth, are not easy riches to find.

Noah and Aurora carefully navigated their way through this minefield, with the objective of uncovering that which had been buried. The relentless search for the truth had been a turbulent process of excavation and discovery. It had been a journey with the objective of reaching a personal viewpoint that made sense, and one placing heavy demand on their intuitive capabilities and faculties of discernment. Ultimately, it was about achieving a spiritually mature perspective in understanding the physical world of matter, and blending this with the comprehension of the non-physical.

Over time, the couple became increasingly familiar with the extent of the deceit, soon realising that what most perceived as reality, was a complete inversion of the truth. The common consensus held amongst society became abhorrent to them. As such, these lone rangers of justice, fostered a righteous reluctance in interacting with this prevailing level of distortion. The level of collective dissonance posed issues in meeting like-minds, and the discordant state of the world rendered them somewhat unwilling to exchange with it too much. Consequently, they imposed limitations upon the regularity and extent to which they interfaced with the outer scape.

It has been said that a period of isolation is invariably a precursor to enlightenment. For this team of truth-seeking nomads, the unmasking of the truth, had coursed them through confronting terrain and at many junctures, they had felt alone in a foreign jungle. Isolation is often experienced by those who choose to stand up and challenge the consensus. They become fringe dwellers, divided from the masses through their refusal to accept the status quo.

Nonetheless, Noah and Aurora had each other, which was all they needed. They enjoyed phenomenal unity on all fronts and were able to make the best of, what was otherwise, an isolated existence from the world at large.

Deciding to treat themselves, the two ventured nearby to a newly opened restaurant, set in the gardens of a beautifully refurbished period mansion. It was a tranquil place to sit, enjoy the sunshine and talk. They loved to converse, for they were best friends, so great discussions were a regular occurrence.

'May we have two glasses, without ice, thank you,' Noah requested, as he sat down and acquainted himself with the surrounds.

'Bottled water, sir?'

The waitress had misconstrued his request. Tap and bottled water had been off the menu for both Noah and Aurora for some time.

'No thank you, just two empty glasses,' replied Noah, holding up their bottle filled with purified water.

The discovery that fluoride, a well documented neurotoxin, was being added to drinking water, had driven the couple into drawing a line in the sand. Many years ago, they had invested in a complete filtration system designed to remove impurities, heavy metals, and most importantly chemicals, such as fluoride. They never left home without their own mineralised and alkalised water — they simply refused to drink anything else. Fluoride had long been totally removed from their life.

The contamination of the water itself, was only one component. Another was the proliferation of plastics, and the fact that they leach harmful toxins, including hormone disrupters, into the water contained. Monopolised by the major corporate entities, this unregulated industry operated without any accountability for the health of their consumers, or regard for the obvious environmental consequences. To that end, Noah and Aurora consciously used only glass vessels, and blue in particular, as per the Hawaiian practice of *Ho'oponopono*.

They had undertaken comprehensive studies on the multi-faceted subject of water, including the work of Masaru Emoto, a Japanese researcher. Emoto's experiments, having not received the accolades they deserved, demonstrated the effect simple energies, like human thoughts, sounds and intentions, have upon the structure of water. This was proof of case enough, that water was particularly responsive to, and affected by energy.

The diverse body of knowledge they'd compiled during their study, was actively integrated into a holistic lifestyle that the couple were gradually formulating. Emoto's work had inspired them to decorate their filter system unit, and glass drinking bottles, with words of positivity and affirmative statements of intention.

Water is an unheralded wonder of creation. As a unique combination of two gases forming a liquid, it is a living energetic element holding a memory of its own and believed to be the most malleable computer known to man. The basic molecules of life (DNA, proteins and cell membranes), could not function without this miraculous substance — it is the essence of human life. When we consider that we are composed of seventy percent water, it makes perfect sense that this element has the capacity to affect overall health and cause major change in our system. Thus, in order to achieve optimum health, the human biological organism relies on regular consumption, and efficient absorption, of organically structured water.

The alterations that the couple had both made over an extended period of time, produced tangible differences; evidenced by improved clarity, an increase in vitality and a progressive enhancement in the faculties of higher sensory perception. These recognisable benefits ignited Aurora's passionate disposition, and she liked to regularly share what she had experienced first hand.

'Remember last week, when I spoke to Isabelle?' said Aurora, recounting her explanation of the chat she had with her client.

'I endeavoured to explain to her that it was no coincidence, that the "8 glasses of water per day" campaign commenced in 1945, the *same* year fluoride was introduced to the water supply!'

Town drinking water supplies across the world, had decades ago, become the vehicle for the negligent and irresponsible disposing of a toxic industrial waste byproduct, originating from the phosphate fertiliser industry. This hazardous and harmful chemical had been monetised and added to the water supplies of unsuspecting human beings, who were encouraged to consume unsafe levels of it, all under the guise of dental health. The modus operandi of this high-level globalist agenda, however, was to further perpetrate the disconnection of the human technology from its connection to source, through the purposeful calcification of the pineal gland.

Aurora tiredly placed her head in her hands at the realisation of the disparity that exists between the truth, and the reality that the majority are aware of, and thus experiencing.

Some concepts, for many, are cognitively impossible to grasp. The truth is simply beyond the comprehension and relative perceptual capacity of most. The programmed mind renders the human being shackled, as the prisoner to an unnaturally diminished level of perceptive ability and manifest experience, limited to the belief in only that which one can see and touch. Those who are indentured to this blindness become the enslaved, bound to an artificially programmed mind.

'That's the problem...,' said Noah, shrugging his shoulders in agreement with Aurora's display of obvious bewilderment.

'It's just so immensely difficult to convey exactly what it's really like to perceive, and feel, through open eyes.' Noah empathetically concluding of those who suffer a dissonance, and are yet to awaken and embark upon the path of truth.

Throughout the generations, the unrelenting level of intrusion, manipulation and inversion of truth, on so many levels of the physical and the non-physical, has served to engineer a hive-mind/groupthink construct. *Repeaters*, like artificially programmed robots, automatically regurgitate propaganda as truth, unaware of just how ignorant they really are. It is a deep sleep state and most detrimental on the physical and spiritual levels. The result is the cyclical reproduction of a hi-jacked, distorted and spiritually disconnected collective consciousness, which unfortunately once again, constitutes the present day majority.

The couple sat together enjoying what were always memorable, colourful and productive conversations about a multitude of different topics. Throughout their journey, both had talked for many hours, and this was to be no exception.

'It's a similar situation when you discuss the nature of reality, the universe and all things supernatural,' said Noah, deciding to slightly change the topic, and take a broader angle.

'So, I'm thinking,' Noah continued, '...if the third dimension is the dimension of matter, the material world, then it must share an intimate relationship with the concept of the three physical dimensions. You know, the three dimensions of shape that give us the perception of form; length, width and depth. When combined we have a three dimensional object.'

'Yes, go on,' replied Aurora.

'I would say, in the comprehension of these concepts, that the third dimensional experience of reality is predominantly occupied with 'things', and the commonplace perception that all that exists are objects that can be seen — three dimensional,' Noah concluded, mindful that Aurora had motioned to add to what he'd been saying.

'Interesting, as it's my understanding that this 3D perceptive lens relates to the root, sacral and solar plexus chakras,' Aurora added, drawing on the knowledge she had accumulated, having comprehensively delved into the subject. She recognised that this projected experience of reality, was intimately connected to the lower aspects of the human chakra system.

Noah excitedly dived back in.

'The lower chakras are the earthly chakras aren't they?'

'Yes, they represent the roots of our own personal existential tree. It is where our eternal consciousness anchors into the physical world, grounding us into the world of matter and the domain of things we can touch, smell and observe.'

Aurora had learnt that the chakras are energetic centres divinely connected to the aether, and that the health and efficient functioning of this system, largely determines our physical state of being. The root chakra, the first, is reputed to represent the aspects of us around survival, security, grounding and community. The sacral chakra being the second, represents sexuality, creativity and emotional stability and the third, the solar plexus, is associated with power, purpose and action.

The fourth dimensional centre, housed within the heart, connects the human being into a higher wavelength band of interaction with the universe. It is the chakra of divine connection, unity, love and compassion. It is the spiritual bridge revealing the higher intelligence fields of source, elevating one out of an experience limited to the 3D. Through an open heart channel, the experience of reality shifts one beyond the perception of simple matter alone. Thus, life experienced through the expanded lens of the heart intelligence, transcends the third dimensional perception of reality, which is governed by the lower three chakras. When one remains centred in the heart, it maintains the connection with the divine soul aspect, whilst at the same time, simultaneously encountering physical world experiences.

Noah attributed the recent uplift in his consciousness as indicative of being more centred in his heart space. The couple discussed the importance of the heart, the fourth chakra, and the liberating role it plays in the human experience. For one cannot transcend the illusion, without piercing the membrane of delusion, moving beyond the third dimension, into the fourth of the heart space. It is from here, that one has the opportunity to ascend into an elevated level of consciousness, where the higher sensory perception is accessible.

'So what of the fifth dimension?' Noah posed.

'Well, from what I understand, if we consistently project our consciousness from the heart space, the experience of true reality can be greatly expanded through the activation of the fifth chakra being the throat, relating to the fifth dimension,' Aurora responded.

'So what you're suggesting is that essentially, a fifth dimensional state of consciousness is available, when one pulls the higher frequency energies down through an activated throat chakra, into the intelligence of the heart chakra?' Noah said, emphasising that the heart acts as the bridge through which consciousness is expanded.

'Yes, and once this is achieved, the higher sensory perception abilities of the sixth chakra, the pineal gland, can then be brought online,' she concluded.

This curious little gland, related to the sixth chakra, is associated with the indigo colour spectrum of frequency. It acts as a direct facilitator of gnosis between the human body existing in the physical world, and the higher aspects of our consciousness stationed in the ethereal realms. It is the perceptive lens through which life is experienced with amplified intuitive power, delivering a deeper, more vivid and advanced perspective.

By design, human beings are genetically coded to be connected to this source domain, through the third eye, without interruption. However, if this crystalline structure is tainted, through over-exposure to neurotoxins, the connection and the innate higher sensory abilities are all but severed. When this is understood, the basis for the post-war strategy to contaminate the water we consume, becomes crystal clear.

Aurora recalled the recent interaction with her client, and how she had informed her of the detrimental affect fluoride has upon the functioning capacity of the pineal. She recounted for Noah how she had made the woman aware of the systematic attack waged upon it, and the challenges most now face in decalcifying it.

'I momentarily witnessed her open up in consideration of the new information I was sharing with her. I also felt that as a consequence, she may perhaps go away and commence her own journey of inquiry.'

Noah listened intently gazing up into the old banyan tree. Aurora referenced how Isabelle appeared to be most perturbed by the disclosure of this conspiracy.

'I had to leave it there. There is a multitude of information accessible, for those curious, courageous, resourceful and industrious enough to seek it out,' Aurora concluded.

It is impossible to impart the holistic view of the truth instantly and succinctly. When people are locked into the personality and ego, in the midst of reconciling the separation, pain and trauma, they are too often confused and bedazzled under the veil of three dimensional life. This results in a total inability to spiritually comprehend the more complex concepts that reside in the realm of the unseen, which can only be felt. It is as though one is, by design, required to undertake and navigate their own passage, through the gathering of knowledge, deeper understanding and wisdom. As such, the individual's return to the truth is always different. It is a process of free will, a non-linear and infinite stream of development, where the value to the soul lies in that which is gained throughout the expansion within the personal journey.

Most, invariably feel the calling to 'the search' at some time in their life, as we all sense that faint thread connecting us to the fabric of our true nature, and the source of our genesis. Our logical human inclination expects to find certainty in unequivocal answers, the discovery of which would mark the completion of the individual search. However, it must be said, that there is no definitive conclusion, nor finale, in the experience and evolution of consciousness, as by nature, both the truth and consciousness are eternally evolving.

Aurora pointed out a bright blue bird rarely seen on the island, the sighting of which acted as a welcome reprieve from the deep conversation they'd been in. The couple sat in sheer silence for some five minutes, observant of the bird's aerial prowess as it dove, and then fossicked about in the garden. It was a fascinating interplay of natural elements to witness; the deep lush greens of the garden, set off by the gentle sounds of running water, and the brilliance of the Indian Roller whose magnificent colour was being exemplified by the illuminating light of the sun.

The rays burst through the banyan tree, and Noah lost track of the bird who had become enticed by the plethora of bugs sitting on the moss. He held his face up toward the sun, so as to soak up the light codes it was emanating that day. For the sun is not only our main source of natural vitamin D, it is a perpetually radiant powerhouse. It emits living solar energy which is transmuted by the Earth, and provides sustenance to all living organisms. For this reason, they both loved to spend days out basking in it. It had always served to boost their mood, energise them, and build a surplus of life force.

In contravention to the indisputable facts, the solar body had been demonised, and humans discouraged from exposure to its vital and benevolent energy. People had been deplorably misinformed, and conditioned to perceive the sun as a threat and something that they should protect themselves from. They were advised to lather their bodies in toxic concoctions, shield their eyes from the ultraviolet rays, and generally avoid exposure to its otherwise beneficial properties.

'Isn't it absurd how propaganda has vilified the sun, yet placed the moon, an artificial satellite, on a pedestal to be worshipped,' Noah remarked.

He was quite horrified with the propensity for which people were inadvertently giving their energy to the moon; an inorganic structure which, through its inversion of natural law, functioned to manipulate the planetary body.

Aurora concurred with Noah's sentiment. She was explicitly aware that this lunar outpost was installed to distort the planet's natural magnetic orientation, and overlay it with an artificial frequency net. As a well informed woman, she knew the chief objective of this moon matrix was to control and suppress human consciousness. Often through her interactions with other women, she felt compelled to bring light to the dark side of the moon, given it was primarily responsible for the desecration of the divine feminine; a well concealed fact, that stood in polar opposition to widely held belief.

In stern protest to this unnatural and entropic intervention, Aurora had righteously refused to partake in the common practice of placing her crystals out in the moonlight, for her natural persuasion had always aligned with charging them in the sunlight. For she had a particular affinity with the sun, having spent the wildly free summer days of her childhood drenched by the sprinkler, beneath the beaming rays in the land down under. Thus, since moving to the tropics, it had come as no surprise, that the consistently bright, warm weather contributed greatly to her state of health.

Most people innately love the sun. It's a deep inner knowing, recorded in the memory of the original earth based DNA, held by the earth's inhabitants. It is by virtue of this natural magnetism, that we are all attracted to sunny destinations, tropical paradises and sun kissed beaches. There is nothing that makes one feel more alive, quite like the feeling of the sun's rays touching our skin, and this is why most seek it out.

On a spiritual level, the perpetuation of paranoia, in relation to the reportedly harmful impacts of the sun, had been geared to discourage the masses from accreting what were progressive waves of incoming plasmic light. For light transmits information, it carries data, coding and downloadable packets that the human organism, and all life within the living library, require to sustain life, elevate in consciousness, and evolve.

The couple's intensive study of consciousness and reality, had served to impart them with much wisdom in terms of the interconnection of all things. For Noah and Aurora, light's relationship to the transmission of information, mirrored the relationship of frequency to energy. Frequency is the language through which energy speaks. It is how energy moves throughout all the realms, creating and supporting life as it flows in wave form.

The earth body has its own frequency, known as the Schumann Resonance. This resonance, likened to the heartbeat of the Earth, measures a set of spectrum peaks in the Earth's electromagnetic field. All sentient beings residing on the planet, resonate with this frequency, and also influence it — just as it influences us.

'Have you checked the Schumann Resonance today?' Noah enquired with Aurora, feeling somewhat hyper-sensitive. His bio-neurological attunement alerted him to the periods when pulses were occurring.

'Yes! There's been a lot of activity overnight and throughout today,' Aurora informed Noah.

Both had often seen correlations with heightened levels of activity, coinciding with observable changes in mood, energy levels and various physical symptoms. In fact, Aurora had discovered that, throughout the days they had been subjected to the *Flu,* the Resonance had simultaneously peaked. This solidified them in the knowledge that their bodies were continuously phasing with these electromagnetic waves. It reinforced the inseparable nature of their relationship with unseen energetics, and conclusively pointed to the fundamental role frequency played in their existence. For these frequencies have an array of impacts on the human electromagnetic field, DNA expression and thus, the overall state of consciousness.

Over the past decade, there had been considerably higher resonance readings reported, with the Schumann spiking, and for prolonged periods of time. It had, for the first time in recorded history, reached frequency levels previously unheard of, and was headed for a maximum spike, equivalent to seven times the base level. This was symptomatic of an evolutionary leap.

Having witnessed this phenomenon, Noah and Aurora intuitively gathered, that the intensity and regularity of these peaks, was indicative of the events that transpire at the end of a cosmic cycle. For fluctuations in this resonance, were influenced by things such as increased solar activity and the precession of the equinoxes.

Mother Earth displays the evidence and the observable signs of change, for those with the eyes to see, and recognise it. As a living consciousness body, she is in direct exchange and interaction with us. She is supporting our journey through the lifting of the veil, toward an inevitable tipping point. The point at which a critical mass of spiritually adept human beings hold the sufficient light frequency quota, whereby they may transition with her, through the zero-point field onto the ascending timeline of evolution.

From the blueprint level, transmissions from the source fields were preparing the collective consciousness for this eventual transit out of the finite temporal planes of third dimensional reality. It was a divine cosmic plan laying the foundation for an upgrade in base frequency. Through the sequential process of incension, the holographic template was to shift from carbon based human order, to the silicate based divine order of multi-dimensionality. The human family, the planet and all life forms would emerge elevated into the infinitely spiritual realm, seated in the fifth dimension. To some, this may sound like an entirely different world, in the physical sense, however, the opposite appears to be the case. The human experience of the physical world remains rooted in the Earth, albeit observed through a lens adorned with greater clarity, and connection to our divine aspects. From this, a vastly different world embodying unity evolves.

The couple sat over what was a lengthy lunch, discussing what they intuitively perceived as living through unprecedented times. Times they foresaw, through the passing of which, would bring immense positive change, ultimately culminating in humankind claiming its rightful place on an emancipated planet. On many levels they sensed, that the world they entered, would not be the same world they would depart.

XVI

PRIMORDIAL SOUND FIELDS

"Sound will be the medicine of the future,"

— *Edgar Cayce*

Having taken in a majestic sunset from the cape, the couple lit candles, gathered their art supplies, and prepared for a therapeutic night in drawing.

Noah decided to put some music on. For him, the themes, messages, stories and the sentiment transmitted through music, proved to hold keys in unlocking his universal self, as much as sound at large, promised to hold the keys to the universe.

They sat down on the sofa, delving into the songs of the 70's and early 80's. Noah was swept away; memories of long trips with his parents, arduous miles of highway, millions of acres of nothingness, across dry and unforgiving terrain. It was a surprising and uplifting exercise, in that he was now viewing the experiences of childhood with enhanced clarity. Listening to the songs, he was able to observe and better understand the formative period, when he was constructing his emotional and mental bodies. The music held the keys to opening the corridors of the past. The songs catapulted him into further insight pertaining to his childhood.

He was blessed with a photographic mind, and the music was now serving as a catalyst for calling back times passed. His ability to recollect with context had been reinstated, which for Noah, was invaluably healing. The lyrics, that he had naturally committed to memory, offered him an expanded window into the deeper contents of his emotional body. Through the coherent resolution of a more spiritually mature lens, he now possessed a greater capacity to consciously interpret the lyrics, and the stories they told.

Noah and Aurora had an affinity with music and knew the benefits of sound, both its ability to moderate and effect mood, and the role it played in raising consciousness. As much as they loved it though, they had become frustrated with the distortion of sound and the manipulation of music by the mainstream music industry. At the fundamental level, it had been nefariously hi-jacked in order to engineer certain designed social outcomes and pathologies.

There had been a strategic militarisation of music worldwide. In 1936, the American standard for tuning was changed to A=440Hz, paving the way for the future monopolisation of music. The imposition of this discordant frequency functions to herd collective consciousness into more aggressive behaviours, psychosocial agitation and regular states of emotional distress. It serves to predispose people to a greater experience of physical illness and general disharmony. Many musicians vehemently oppose the industry standard (ISO) of 440Hz as a reference for tuning, in fact they consider it to be an abomination of nature. Regardless, virtually all commercially produced contemporary music is tuned to this standard.

This annoyed Noah and Aurora greatly. For not only had the purity of music, in terms of subject matter and the content, been corrupted, but over time the frequency of music itself had been rendered down to a point of gross dissonance. Most disturbed by the level of interference, they refused to listen to modern music at all, except on the seldom occasion. When they did, they much preferred songs by the musicians of yesteryear, back when the music was raw, heartfelt, more artistic, less adulterated and centred around the showcasing of the voice and instruments. Melodies that were composed by talented artists, who for the most part, told their stories through lyrics that were wholesome, meaningful and uplifting. It was music devoid of overtly sexual connotation, synthetic sound and the hypnotic, trance-like properties characteristic of modern music.

It had been a fortuitous experience, that when walking through a small countryside town in Spain one afternoon, they made acquaintance with a local busker. They spent an hour soaking up the soulful sounds emanating from the man's flamenco guitar. Such was his talent, that once he'd finished, the couple decided to gift him a generous donation. The eccentric man, ever so grateful, then struck up some interesting conversation. The like-mindedness they shared was particularly refreshing. A lengthy discussion ensued across an array of topics, the most prominent was around the benefits of tuning music to specific frequencies. He had shared how music makers like himself, were headlining a musical revolution with the aim of advancing world peace and health. They were retuning their instruments to *'Verdi's A'* (A=432Hz), assuring they would perform optimally, impact audiences more beneficially and restore integrity to the performing arts. The greatest advice the musician had given them, was the existence of software which allowed the user to tune music to their preferred frequency tone.

This had changed the game significantly, and allowed Noah and Aurora to comfortably listen to their favourite songs and enjoy the seldom trips down memory lane. They had experimented with the application many times. It involved playing music in the standard 440Hz, and then adjusting it to 432Hz. The differences were astounding. The music in 432Hz was vibrant and emotive, the 440Hz rendition was dull and lifeless. This proved the capacity for music to deliver notable variations in experience. Based on these comparisons, Noah concluded that sound did indeed hold both the power to heal, and likewise the capacity to inflict harm.

Human consciousness is intrinsically related to sound. Our cells respond to vibration and frequency, altering our inner landscape, and so too, our outer landscape. As evidenced by the study of cymatics, when we utilise sound waves such as harmonious music, words or tones that feel positively resonant in the cells of our body, we automatically increase inner harmony and coherence, which greatly strengthens our spiritual and physical immunity. The frequency of 432Hz is resonant with the macrocosm, and the microcosm; it has a pure tone of math, fundamental to nature. It is therefore, mathematically consistent with the patterns of the universe, connected to everything from nautilus shells, to the works of the ancients, including the construction of the Great Pyramid. Herein, lies its ability to transmit such beneficial healing energy.

Aurora took a break from her artwork, and prepared a pot of tea in the kitchen. As she waited for the chamomile leaves to steep, she sung her heart out across the apartment. She innately knew of the unsung benefits of singing. It is a great mechanism to relieve the body of stress and anxiety, bringing on feelings of euphoria and pleasure, through its release of oxytocin and endorphins. When she sang, it was in the full embrace of her personality and zest for life.

She had always gravitated to the power of music. Growing up Aurora had applied herself studiously in learning to play the grand piano. At the beginning of their relationship, she'd sit and play for Noah, enchanting him with her sweet renditions of the classics. She shared this mutual passion for music with her grandfather, Dino. Under his watchful eye, she had taught herself to play a few songs on an instrument traditional to his village in Italy. When he passed, he bequeathed the custom made organetto to her, in recognition of her appreciation for it. Since she'd departed the homeland, she dearly missed these instruments, stored some six thousand kilometres away.

There was only so long she would go, without playing an instrument, as for Aurora, playing was therapeutic, and the instruments were a vehicle through which she creatively expressed. So, somewhat by necessity, she adopted a more convenient instrument in the form of a travel-sized ukulele; a handy accompaniment on their journey throughout the world. She learnt all she set her disciplined mind to with ease, affording her a capacity to learn new things quickly, and as such in the case of music, she now possessed a well trained ear.

Being so musically oriented, Aurora had vigorously questioned the efficacy of any digital music, particularly given her knowledge of the now compromised state of music generally. Moreover, for Aurora, nothing quite matched the sound of musical instruments manufactured from natural materials, such as wood, reeds, metals, animal hides and fibres. Instruments handmade from these materials generate pure unadulterated sound; sounds that align with nature and produce positive affects on the mind, body and spirit.

'We should book in for a session at the sound healing centre tomorrow,' Aurora announced.

Noah emphatically agreed with the timely suggestion and reserved two spots in the following days group sound bath. It was to be the second occasion that they would visit the centre. The first visit had entailed an hour long private session entranced by the Tibetan singing bowls. Both were quite surprised at just how much clearer, more refreshed and energised they were afterward — this modality had sincere merit.

Aurora took a deep breath, having just completed her intricate and colourful mandala, imprinted with a personal creative signature. The couple loved creating mandalas, it served as a tool through which they transposed the contents of their inner sanctum onto paper. She held it up proudly for Noah to see, and he complimented her on what was a beautiful expression of harmonious geometry.

The time had flown by and it was getting late. They packed up their supplies, tidied the apartment and turned in for the evening, listening to the second movement in Beethoven's 7th Symphony.

Having slept solidly the couple rose early. Noah fixed breakfast, and then they decided to venture down in the general direction of the sound healing centre. Given the session was scheduled for early afternoon, they figured they'd take advantage of the beautiful weather, and lay out on the beach for a couple of hours.

Arriving for the session early, they walked the tropical garden surrounding the main therapy space. It was a serene, oxygen dense and peaceful sanctuary, attracting butterflies, birds, bees and a multitude of other life. The owners, Otto and Flow, had done a wonderful job respecting the natural habitat, leaving much of the plant life that thrived on the land, untouched.

Otto conducted and facilitated the sound sessions with trademark German precision, alongside his wife, Flow, a mild mannered, kind and graceful local woman. The centre was a celebration of their intense passion for sound healing, with the venture representing an exciting new chapter in a journey they shared together.

There was quite a buzz in the air as the participants slowly arrived for a 3:30pm start. Some milled around, sipping on the lemon water provided, and some explored the cute little shop that sold crystals, textiles, singing bowls along with other handmade items that Otto brought back from his twice yearly pilgrimage to Nepal.

When it came time for the sound bath, Flow rang the chirpy little Tibetan bell, ushering the small group of twelve toward the main room. It was a diverse group that had congregated; some were local, some foreign, some cynical and some excited. They made their way up the steps, placed down their belongings, removed their shoes and entered the reposeful room.

Noah and Aurora paused, taking in the fascinating space. It had an unmistakable presence, one of a pure healing space operated by practitioners that were loving and in complete integrity.

The room had an inviting warmth and was delightfully ambient. Washed stone walls featured mandalas and various prints; one detailing the history of the healing modality, and another depicting the human body in relation to the chakra system. Abundant natural light flowed in through prodigious windows which were left ajar, and Tibetan prayer flags swayed gently in the breeze. Small hand-stitched Nepalese blankets and pillows were meticulously set out, on the rich timber floorboards, framing the perimeter of the space. At the far end, resting on little velvet pads, were a grand arrangement of singing bowls, each waiting patiently for their magic to be brought to life.

Singing bowls have a long and revered history. The sensory deluge they supply, delivers an acutely spiritual experience for the receiver. They are wonderful tools in repairing, activating and harmonising the physical body with the non-physical auric layers. Noah enjoyed the sound of the bowls, and had always had a particular resonance with the one tuned to the heart chakra. He recalled having bought one some fifteen years prior, and tried to recall when he'd misplaced it.

Having chosen a spot closest to the bowl arrangement, the couple laid down and got themselves comfortable. The session commenced and the two focused on their breathing as directed, peacefully drifting off into a state of deep relaxation immersed in the sounds.

Sometime midway through the procession of the bowls, the frequency adopted a noticeable change. Noah sensed a powerful and instantaneous energetic transition, from the solar plexus to the heart. His throat became engorged and it was becoming hard to swallow. It was the type of choking up that often precedes a great emotional emancipation of some kind. Suddenly, a glistening, glowing coppery white light appeared with brilliant dynamic vibrance, totally encompassing his inner field of sight. An explosive surge of gut wrenching emotion burst forth and streams of uncontrollable tears flowed from his eyes. He was emotionally exposed, feeling somewhat uneasy in the moment, not knowing whether Otto or any of the other participants were aware of his state. Without the ability to repress it, Noah surrendered to a cascade of tears. In that moment, he was open to accepting that there was likely still remnants of debris and old dark miasma there to be exorcised.

Once the session concluded, each person took the time they needed to 'come back to Earth,' before gathering their belongings. Noah having pulled himself together, glanced over at the clock noticing the time as 4:44pm.

Otto thanked the attendees, informing them of another group session scheduled for the same time the following week. Flow encouraged the group to stay on, mingle and share their experiences, directing them to the area overlooking the garden where refreshments would be served.

Noah and Aurora were elated to see the assortment of delicious raw cakes and organic fresh fruit. As Noah surveyed the choices, taking a piece of the coconut slice, one of the participants caught his eye. The man stood alone, unassuming, as he sipped on his fresh ginger and lime tea.

Noah didn't take to many people. It wasn't that he was reserved, but more so that, in order to be sociable, he needed to sense resonance and a gravitational pull. He was sensitive and attuned to the vibrational signature of people. These innate persuasions had often worked against him, as it tended to compound his sense of isolation and 'differentness' over the years.

Noah observed a particularly mature, sophisticated and balanced energy around the man, which stirred his interest. He intuited that perhaps some meaningful banter would ensue, if he only made the effort to break the ice. Noah relayed a friendly smile, so as to make a connection. Deciding to be proactive (a working motto since the days of the *Flu)*, Noah elected to approach the man. He offered his right hand and exchanged the commonplace greetings.

Antonio was his name. He was an Englishman, an expatriate who had lived abroad for some ten years. He brandished the steeliest of blue eyes, conveyed an air of astuteness, with a manner of speaking that portrayed a knowledgeable, symbiotic and gnostic disposition.

Having passed the stage of the generic discoveries around name and origin, Noah enquired as to what work Antonio did. The man proceeded to shorthand his life, his impressive studies, his colourful journey and his high level of understanding in the domain of fundamental spiritual mysteries.

Noah being the conscientious type, was feeling fortunate to be interfacing with what was obviously an elevated level of wisdom. He listened intently, for he was a good listener, and normally only spoke when he had something worthwhile to say.

Antonio had spent many years studying meditation and was proficient in many different techniques. Blended with this knowledge was a deep understanding of human psychology, thus his specialisation had become the ability to teach people to quieten, harness and master their minds.

This sparked Noah's interest, as over the last three years he had more routinely allocated time each day to meditation. Noah recognised that the breath was the vehicle through which one may establish a stronger connection to the true nature of all things. It was a quintessential practice in the process of ascension toward the realms of enlightenment. For in reality, the inhalation of the inward breath represents receiving, the feminine principle, and the exhalation of the outward breath is representative of giving, the masculine principle — this is the balance of the divine.

Noah listened attentively, as he assessed the man to be quite unique and a great teacher. Despite Antonio's level of gnosis, the conveyance of his message was marvellous in its simplicity. He had a way of making the complex readily understandable. He explained that the breath was an invaluable tool in attaining the level of clarity that many seek, primarily due to the fact that with practice, one becomes better able to settle the over-active subconscious mind.

Antonio conveyed that it was all about acknowledging its presence, but then quietening its voice, in order to simply bring the focus of attention down to only that of the inhalation and the exhalation. It is at this point that balance may be achieved by the meditator. This is the space where the perceptions of self are dispelled, and one subtly merges with the greater whole. It is at this intersection that the mind, body and spirit are unified.

The exchange excited Noah greatly, and prepared him to venture onward, forging a more informed and purposeful exploration in the attainment of this unified state of being; where one embodies the truth in wholeness, released of any separation or polarity.

Division, separation and the spiritual schism characterising inner polarity, sees a person detached from themselves, humanity and their cosmic surroundings. This breeds and spreads as a regressing infestation, creating a barrier to the achievement of a harmonious relationship between the mind, body and spirit. It is an energetic contagion. From a state of individuated spiritual dis-ease, it then radiates outwardly seeding its discordant energetics, making an adverse energetic contribution which directly affects the health of the planet and all its inhabitants, as all is interconnected. From the level of person, into the collective level, into the planetary level and out into the universe, this small seed of infection swiftly germinates into a larger and malignant energetic body, a universal *Spiritual Flu*.

Noah and Aurora sought out Otto, thanked him, and said their goodbyes. Otto made a point of giving thanks to the couple, as their review of their first visit was so positive, it had helped to increase the numbers attending the day's session. Aurora enquired about the possibility of a private session in a month's time, to which Flow replied, that it wouldn't be possible.

'I'm sorry, we won't be here as we are heading off to Nepal again next week...,' advised Flow.

'Where?' Noah posed, having overheard what Flow had said to Aurora.

'We're going back to Kathmandu for the second time this year. We're going to do more advanced training with the master of the singing bowls,' Flow said.

Noah quickly turned to look at Aurora with bulging eyes, as though what he had just heard was astonishing.

He thanked them again for the fantastic session, before returning to the car.

'That's it. That's the place...we're going, and we're going this year, let's book it,' Noah hastily announced.

'Okay, okay...we'll go,' replied Aurora, accommodatingly. She understood exactly why he had reacted the way he had. She knew he had aligned with an obvious synchronicity.

'That's the place the card reader at the market was talking about — the place I need to go to.'

It felt right. He wanted to begin planning as soon as possible. Such was his enthusiasm, he immediately started to discuss the logistics on the drive home. Without argument, Aurora agreed they should go; she also felt a magnetic pull, knowing full well that the language of the universe speaks to us through signs. They had both been savouring the symphonic presentation of symbols and the divinely orchestrated way their days had been unfolding.

Having calmed Noah's enthusiasm somewhat, Aurora changed the topic of conversation to that of her reflections on the afternoon. She made comment as to what a nice experience it had been at the centre, and how refreshing it was to interact with people of like mind. Both concurred that in recent times, when they talked to people, they regularly found themselves conversing about things more spiritually oriented, meaningful and positive in nature.

As these interactions became more commonplace, Noah and Aurora sensed the imminence of an awakening, and on a global scale. There was evidence that the frequency was incrementally lifting, and that suggested the world was in the active process of change, and for the better. People were becoming increasingly more curious, about much in life; the pursuit of happiness, the nature of reality, the purpose of human existence, true history and the structure of the universe. The same core set of topics always seemed to come up for discussion. People were gradually beginning to seek answers to the big questions, to bravely explore each and every pixel in a chaotic, confusing, inverted and nonsensical reality. They were collecting the knowledge by finding the pieces of the puzzle, pieces that when placed together eventually illuminate the truth, as a fully discerned and coherent image — the artwork of awakening.

The following morning Noah woke early with the sunrise. He was keen to begin making investigations into Nepal's historical landmarks and places of interest, along with checking the availability of flights, with a view to planning out the trip.

Adventurous in spirit, both had always dreamed of visiting places of planetary significance like Machu Picchu, the pyramids and the Mayan ruins, particularly the Gateway Arch. However, their cold and dreary hometown had starved them of sunlight, and with limited vacation time they had chosen to holiday almost exclusively in the tropics — such was their desire for the sun and the sea. Now residing near the equator, where the days were consistently warm and bright, they were afforded new flexibility in what type of adventure they would consider embarking on. This was a unique opportunity to explore a destination, that they would have in the past, overlooked. In this case, and under the circumstances, both had agreed it was an opportune time to simply move with the tide and just do it.

Whilst the timing of the trip was best set for October, it posed a potential clash with Pamela arriving for her second annual visit. Considering that she was so very understanding, Noah hadn't a worry, figuring that she'd be untroubled by a change of dates. What he was slightly concerned about though, was the likelihood of having to withstand the motherly commentaries regarding the spontaneous need to travel — questions about motivations, cost and the need to take leave from work. These were however, all things the couple would carefully consider of their own accord.

'I have to inform Mum of our plans, so she can adjust her travel dates. I don't want to inconvenience her by notifying her too late...'

Noah called his mother.

'Hi, is everything okay?' Pamela answering the phone with an all too regular question, which slightly irritated Noah, as it carried an air of pessimism. Nonetheless, Noah exercised tolerance, understanding that it came from a mother's genuine concern for her child. She loved both of them unconditionally and this was only highlighted in what transpired.

'We're going to Nepal, Mum...in October. I have to go, it will be the finale to my book...oh yes, I haven't told you yet. I'm writing a book, I've written one-hundred-and-forty-four pages already, and it's going to be a great success.'

Pamela decided to postpone her trip for a few months. She had instinctively felt that, for the couple, the trip would be one of great significance. She also saw another benefit and thus expressed a wish for the couple to 'take some time.' The last months and years had been tumultuous — both the highs and the lows, the quest to become parents, the consequential disappointments, the virus and the observable newness in her son's entire being.

'Okay, well if that's so, I'd like to pay for it, okay?'

Noah had expected to confront some resistance to both the intended trip, and to the idea of the book, but given the gloriously flowing nature of his life, he could only smile at his goddess, and thank his nurturing mother on the other side of the world for her generosity; it was generosity born of the heart and a maternal unconditional love in abundant kindness.

The trip, fully funded by Pamela, was booked the next week. Return airfares for two, and accommodation for ten nights in a guesthouse recommended by Otto, situated right in the heart of Kathmandu.

XVII

THE INTERSECTION OF RELAPSE
AND THE NOW

With all the excitement surrounding the synchronous mention of Nepal, Noah hadn't much time to reflect on the happenings of the sound session itself. Antonio had left an indelible mark on him, and the imaginings of visiting the mystical destination had encompassed his mind. There was, however, still another profound occurrence for Noah to investigate. It related to the monumental purge he'd encountered during the session, which he hadn't explored, having been so swept up in the other revelations of the day.

Noah focused his enquiries into the possible nature of the copper light he'd witnessed, and the interpreted meanings historically associated with that colour signature. He also asked questions of the universe, requesting that he be furnished with insight into the supernatural encounter. He trusted that whatever information was fitting for him would materialise in perfect timing, knowing full well that everything he experienced had reason and purpose.

Something that had intrigued Noah, was the constant feeling of central compression in his skull, in the location where the pineal gland resides, hidden away from the world. His vision had since taken on enhanced capability, and he noticed he was able to view objects in the distance with far greater resolution — there was more detail to be observed, and accentuation in colour. It was as if he was now perceiving the external world with the benefit of a super modified sense, a sixth sense.

Out on the balcony, he looked down towards the ground level, contemplating the meaning of the emanation that had completely encompassed his session. In that moment, he was surprised by his simultaneous observation of an inscription on a navy blue cap, worn by a teenager some forty meters away. It boldly displayed in heavy white stitching, the letters 'GBL.' From this, Noah immediately intuited the name, *'Gabriel'* — it was a sign, the answer that Noah had asked for, so clearly and eloquently returned back to him through universal language. He felt an instantaneous resonance with the clue and sat with it. For Noah was relatively familiar with the angelic archetypes and the attributes of the seven Arch-Angels; a fundamentally distorted misrepresentation of numerous identities, popularised by the New Age. In the narratives of the Christian religion, Gabriel was reportedly the messenger of God bringing knowledge. He was fabled as sitting alongside Michael in the angelic realm, and purported to have advised Mary of her impending pregnancy with the son of God. According to some Islamic scholars, Gabriel accompanied Muhammad as he ascended to Heaven from the The Dome of The Rock. It was further suggested that Gabriel had taken Muhammad to the rock to pray with Abraham, Moses and Jesus. It is said that Gabriel comes with the message that when one eliminates dark thoughts from the mind and heart, one can finally see more clearly again. This was divine confirmation. Noah knew without a shadow of a doubt that Gabriel was with him. He had presented as a symbol of guidance, new beginnings, clarity and purity.

Everyday in the now, promised new horizons with which to explore and discover. He now viewed each day as having brilliant potential for him, in stark contrast to the days that simply rendered themselves as no more than a repeat of the last. For Noah, the old days represented the depressing regularity of sameness, when he was haunted by an inability to make the changes he desperately desired. The experience of life had forged many negative impositions, and there was always an over-bearing subconscious mind, forever getting in the way. He had frustrated on the wastage of his talent and his inability to reach any sort of contentment. He grappled with not unduly burdening Aurora through his inability to release the pain, guilt and trauma, for she deserved his best. Since he'd known her, he had existed as an irritated and diminished product of his past, but no longer. He had navigated his way out of the metaphysical death passage that had begun in childhood, through a prolonged process of programming, and the subsequent development of his identity, personality and belief systems. As each day drew to a close, it was another triumphant marker in the reckoning stage of his life. It had been a difficult road, and he had regularly questioned whether he possessed fortitude enough to withstand the persistent undulation. At many, many junctures it was a lonely path to walk, an anxiously heartbreaking and apparently futile path. But he had kept the faith, and overcame his challenges, always believing that he would eventually reach a unified state of being. The pursuit of enlightenment requires unwavering focus, commitment, dedication, discernment and coherence. It demands one remain steadfastly cognisant of the universal law of energetics, in that, where attention goes, energy flows. It commands us to seat our consciousness in each now moment, for a lapse in attention allows the automatic mind to rise to prominence again, sprinkling fear, dread and worry, compromising one's entire state of being.

Noah had woken up feeling strangely anxious, tired and disillusioned — the momentum had halted. Was this the end of a short-lived new era, after only a matter of weeks feeling reborn? Was he malignant again? He had fallen into a state of descension, spiralling back into that old version of himself again. This was not his optimal expression, the one that approached each moment, each day and the future as a wonderfully vivid adventure. In a panic, he sensed that he wouldn't be able to face the people at work. He was exposed and vulnerable, a state which he had become accustomed to, prior to the episode of the *Flu*. He wrote, but not for the book he was deeply entrenched in writing; but for help, for attention and from the sub conscious depths that housed the ghosts of his past. It was a pure and unadulterated purge of the still lingering rotten fruits there to be disposed. He purged the remaining contents that had been encased within the structure of his 3D personality matrix, and the counter-productive negative ego construct.

Thrust into total disarray, he fired off a worrisome message, first to his Mother, and then the same to Aurora.

"In actual fact I have had an epiphany in relation to the theme of my book. It's going to be called, 'I'm Broken'
"This is the perfect title for me, as I am fractured. I'm an emotional write off. I have too many regrets, I hold too much resentment, and I can never find any peace.

*I am unstable, tired and I don't want to work. I do not
like the job I do any longer and I have no interest in
doing it anymore. I just want to write. I want to feel like
I am happy for once, inside myself.*

*I do not own a home, or have a place to call my own.
Instead I live on borrowed time in a place I find totally
chaotic. I cannot find any peace here on this planet, only
white noise. This is not what I imagined, I am lost in this
place.*

*I'm a total failure who has destroyed every relationship
I've had. My own child hates me. I've never been able to
get over the pain of the ones I've lost to this evil life.*

*I'm stressed and I worry a lot. I worry that I will be left
alone, and I don't feel that I can look after myself.*

*I am totally screwed up. I sabotage everything I touch.
I am a pain to be around and I'm selfish.*

*I will speak to those like myself, who are too much of a
burden to themselves, too much a product of the past, too
scared of the future — because this is me, so I have no
right to speak to anyone. I am a liability to all of you."*

Pamela swiftly called Aurora to enquire as to the
mental health of her son.

Had he relapsed? Had he faltered in his efforts to
remain in the quantum flow? It appeared so. But these
relapses, these echoes from the past, do continue to rear
their heads, as a catalyst for healing any unresolved pain,

fear and trauma in order to move onward and upward along the path to enlightenment.

Darkness exists only in the absence of light. The shadow we carry as spiritual baggage is the metaphysical pain body, perpetuated and largely characterised, by our level of resistance to the light. It is this resistance that must be acknowledged, absolved and transcended, before the full light of spirit can once again take residence. Each time a remnant aspect of the remaining shadow surfaces, seeking healing through reconciliation, it must be closely monitored, carefully managed and observed without judgement. These are the debilitating and uncomfortable battles that greet us along the path that leads to an eventual state of inner harmony. This is how transformational purification, restoration, resurrection and the potential for full embodiment takes place.

Admittedly, human life has been a difficult undertaking for those who seek to reclaim their truth. Many digress during their incarnation, concerned only with the mundane, remaining unconcerned with innate spiritual purpose. The enslavement matrix enforces this entrapment into disconnection, and many submit to apathy and convenience, succumbing to the suppression and the repression of the dense environment that presides. Furthermore, many perceive life based on linear terms as though there is a distinct beginning, and a distinct end, a transit from an A, to a B — as in from birth to death. However, mortal death only signifies a passing out of the body, an instantaneous shift into another station of awareness, just as it had occurred at the time of birth, the time of transduction. For consciousness is preciously eternal, and thus, so are we. We are eternally magnificent spiritual beings with unlimited potential, and at this level, there is no beginning and no end, there just *is*.

Noah's surrender to the shadow, signalled that he had made a profound shift and reached a point of liberating transition. It represented the piercing of the stubborn membrane sealing the personality matrix, associated with the first, second and third chakras. It served as a reminder that the journey is never over, that the point at which we are to stop working, stop climbing and stop aspiring, never comes. For the pursuit of enlightenment is a journey that commands we respectfully, and reverently, dedicate the totality of consciousness in navigating.

Aurora spent hours counselling Noah. He needed an intensive dose of love, compassion and stern reassurance, as what he'd slipped into, was quicksand to his soul's best expression, unless he promptly fought his way out of it.

Noah sequestered the presence of the panther in all his waking hours. *Kirrah* became a permanent fixture by his side. It was as though the cat gifted him a second set of super eyes through which he could revision the world. For Noah, *Kirrah* symbolised his strong will, and was a guardian of his safety and protection. It brought him comfort and security in marching forth into a new way of being, one that composed a symphony of increased awareness, joy and a deeper, more congruent spiritual experience. Noah had realised the profound importance of his elegant friend and the influence this guide could have in his quest for oneness.

Gabriel also stood by his side. Noah gave daily thanks for this blessing, and for the information transmitted from the aether, that he was now committed to following. For he came to realise that in many instances over the years of his life, he had transgressed against his guardian angels. These were valuable spiritual relationships worth rebuilding through constant commune. Thus, each morning and evening entailed the habitual practice of tuning in and thanking Gabriel, Solar Christ Michael, Joseph and Ninny for their love and guidance, and for keeping him eternally safe and protected.

With regard to his beloved grandmother, Ninny, he had been striving toward a total reconfiguration of his relationship with her eternal presence. Since her death, he had stubbornly, and somewhat naively, held onto the mere mortal version of her. He had refused to accept her death and let her go. He hung onto the pain and the grief associated with her leaving him deserted on this planet.

The time had come for him to face the truth, that she had in fact, departed the physical plane. The signs had come. For Ninny loved cats, and cats soon appeared for Noah everywhere, not just in the dream spaces. Noah saw these as tangible signs of her divine presence. Additionally, since her passing, feathers had regularly fallen at his feet, reminding him of her. They became symbolic of her love. He unequivocally knew, it was his grandmother placing them in his wake.

Following the nightly gestures of gratitude to his guardians, he heard her voice whisper -

'It is time now to take me back into your heart.'

Realising that she was just as present, as in the times when she had been embodied on Earth, Noah was finally ready to accept her back into his life. This was a shift of epic proportions, releasing the grief and the pain, bringing closure to the black memories of her shock death. It fertilised a new relationship with her as infinite consciousness, a soul family elder, and a true guide.

In the consequential process of healing his past, Noah became intensely driven to seek the forgiveness of people close to him, that he felt he had transgressed against. He decided he would make some confronting, yet long overdue admissions. The passing of both Ninny and his step-father in such quick succession, had triggered his fears of abandonment and sent Noah into a free fall, capitulating into an emotional chasm. As such, he had prioritised his own needs, which unfortunately left his mother to process her grief alone. He drafted a message, asking for forgiveness -

"Dear Mum, I wish to offer my heartfelt apology for causing you pain. I left you emotionally unsupported when both your mother, and then Joseph, passed away. I request your loving forgiveness, and seek your advice as to how I may make it up to you."

Pamela's reply granted Noah supreme closure, and the alleviation from a skeleton of the past -

"Wow, I felt that this needed an immediate reply. I can feel how much soul searching you must have done recently, as this admission of how you feel you didn't support me must have been buried deep within your subconscious. I know how devastating the passing of my mother was for you...and you, as we all do at times of loss, needed to grieve in your own way. Sometimes, and I believe this to be true for you at the time of her death, being around others and having no way of easing their grief, only intensifies our own. When Joseph passed I think we were all still numb from Mum, as both losses were so close together. Both changed my world

dramatically, but at no time did I ever say, or think, that you were not there for me. You may not have always been at home, but you were finding your way to cope. You have always been a champion for my welfare, and I know you would protect me from harm, as would I for you. Unfortunately, the downside of loving deeply, is hurting deeply when that love is physically removed, and we were shocked to our core with the loss of two important people, being ripped away so quickly and unexpectedly. You have no need to feel guilt or regret around this, let it be in the past. You have always had, and will always have, my unconditional love. You, nothing, no-one, or any event, will ever change that."

This served to relieve a tremendous amount of guilt, however, there was more where that resided. There was the guilt around leaving his son. A personal message was composed to James, and offered in the faint hope of forgiveness. No reply eventuated from the boy now studying law at university.

The couple's perception and experience of time had significantly changed of recent, compared to what they were accustomed to. Generally, time appeared to have widened, and it was as though they had been granted more time within a regular day to do more, achieve more and become more. Their days took on a revived stature. Early rising, morning meditation, smudging of their space followed by yoga and home-cooked meals together. It set the scene for a productive day, a day which incorporated new discipline.

Noah's body returned to a stronger, more robust stature. The daily practice of yoga had provided the ideal platform for conscious movement and mindful re-strengthening. This practice is precipitated by the idea that one is to work with the body, rather than on the body. It was the first time Noah experienced symbiosis in movement, bridging the body with the mind and the spirit. He admired the practice's ability to re-instate the flow of *prana,* it was an energy he could readily observe flowing up and down his spine following each session.

The more time that elapsed, the further away Noah moved from the past nagging anxieties, the worries over the future, the fears of being left alone and the lack of true passion. He prayed that this lighter way of being in the flow would last, waking each morning checking in to ascertain if the anxiety had returned, if melancholy threatened to ruin his day — and it didn't. Only vague shadows of those times surfaced, which were connected to the great emotional pain related to his son.

Days, then weeks passed by, without sign of the burdensome weight of days gone by. The momentum continued, and he actively fortified this new way of being. It was a holistic state of integration and of real progress.

The old version of Noah had died during the voracious stage of the *Spiritual Flu,* the time at which it took malignant stature. He had shed that skin, and purged the past. He had now also faced off with his shadow. The period of steady awakening seemingly agitated by the *Flu,* had placed him on an upward trajectory, and into remission. That testing day, when he slid back and purged the negativity, was the day his ego died.

Finally, Noah had taken control of the quest, and became the conscious observer in his desire to gain mastery over his mind. Moment by moment he was acutely observant of his thought process, and diligent in his efforts to quieten the penetration of his automatic subconscious mind and negative ego. These two foes had hijacked him for far too long, and it was exclusively Noah's role now to course his own fate.

Noah and Aurora maintained a disciplined regime of meditation. For Noah, this had become the key to happiness, to contentment and to creating an inner world that broadcasted positivity to the aether. He practiced visualisation, perceiving himself in a future reality, as an accomplished author signing books, and attending events where he was commissioned to speak. He visualised his book cover as a large poster hanging behind the table at which he sat, as he introduced himself to readers, inscribing personal messages in autographed copies. He was a man confident in his craft, an author and an accomplished one at that. He placed a strict focus on the feeling of what it was like to have achieved success, in the pursuit of his passion for writing. He brought these feelings into his heart space where the energies of self-love, gratitude, acceptance and connection to purpose reside. This was Noah's best soul expression, a man that had integrated his true self with pure divine purpose.

Persistence had paid off. He had unlocked his potential, and released himself into the space where, as the master of his own destiny, he was cultivating a better future. The days continued to take form unlike they had ever before. He was the neutral observer of the world, perceiving of it differently, and projecting upon it a redefined version of life. There he was, no longer the disillusioned shadow of his potential, aimlessly staring into space on a balcony. It amazed him that he could sit on that same balcony, looking at the same things and yet the experience of what he saw, and how he felt about it, had completely shifted. He had ascended into the heart space. This is the space where birds are observed for their magnificent freedom and flight, where trees are viewed as unique from one another; it is a space where one appreciates the differences, and thanks them for their grand contribution in the cycle of the natural world.

His higher base frequency seemed to attract more interesting birds and insects to the balcony, ones he'd never before seen. As like a child, he stopped and wondered over flowers that he passed by on the street, investigating their spiral like forms. Coincidences, synchronicities, signs and symbols had been the driving force in affirming that he was aligned with the cosmic flow.

Numbers appeared, 4s, everywhere. 4:44pm again, just like the 4:44am of the insomnia ridden period prior to the expulsion of the *Spiritual Flu*. Messages from friends and acquaintances would arrive, synchronously, at 4:04pm and 4:44pm. Numbers on the clothing of people, of battery charge, receipts, street signs and on the license plates of cars passing by. Life was a procession of fours.

This was the symbology of interconnection and flow observed from the higher state of awareness. The numbers were serving a specific purpose — to consolidate an ever increasing confidence. Through the experience of each coincidence, he only felt more and more integrated into the natural flows of the universal mind. It was to move with the tides, rather than clumsily swim against them.

Threes followed, 3:00pm, three people, three on a billboard, threes were everywhere to be seen. When the succession of threes came, Noah immediately cast his mind to the three Musketeers.

Additionally, in the aftermath of the feral plague, Aurora's powerful psychic abilities progressively rose to prominence with amplified acuity. She was coded with natural clairvoyance, and had always carried a gift for lucid dreaming. Ever since the *Flu*, she was more frequently receiving clearer messages, and quite prophetic information about the future.

The couple basked in the quantum flow of energy, delighting in the momentum that they now felt. They looked toward the pilgrimage to Nepal with enormous anticipation. Noah expected the trip to be the pinnacle of his newly expanded way of living, in a world he had finally discovered his contented place within.

Kathmandu, set in the valley beneath Mount Everest, the greatest peak on Earth, is a place of high frequency. A place esteemed for its healing energies, its power and serenity. It is the place where humanity's intrepid explorers gather, before bravely setting off into the great unknown, in one of the most revered tests of human ability, tolerance, courage and determination. The ascent to the summit of this mountain, speaks directly to the overcoming of core human fears. The profound sense of achievement when successful, epitomises one who has risked their own mortality, overcome altitude, the elements, and themselves, to earn the right to stand for a fleeting moment atop the world.

These moments mirrored the moments when travellers would sit a front the sphinx, wander through the expansiveness of the great Angkor Wat temple and soak in the views from Glastonbury Tor — these sacred sites were all places of great energetic significance. They hold a power, a prominent vibration, that emits astoundingly transformational frequencies, leaving visitors forever altered. We gravitate to, and align with these places, as we are fundamentally interconnected with the planet. For it is in our reflection Mother Earth takes shape, maintains life and evolves through her own system of chakras. As part of her foundational energetic make up, each of these chakras, like parts, connect through a sophisticated system of channels, referred to as leylines. At key locations across the globe, these lines intersect and are the junctions at which concentrated and powerful energies culminate. This is why the seekers are drawn; the sense of something larger, the potential to viscerally connect and integrate with something greater than the material world.

Vibrational therapies had taken a prominent role in the couple's life over recent weeks, with additional time being apportioned to sound therapy. Otto, the sound healer, had been gracious enough to refer Noah and Aurora to a great friend, and mentor, of his in the valley. The evidenced healing power of sound, motivated them to enrol in coursework with the Swami, who was a master of the Tibetan singing bowls. Swami, amongst his other business ventures, managed a boutique guesthouse in Kathmandu, right in the thick of the action. Otto had been able to secure the couple privileged rates for a room situated at the back of the building; it was to provide them with a quiet outlook, boasting a stunning view of one of the country's ten World Heritage sites.

Noah was counting down the days until departure. It would be the final break they would share together, before commencing an imminent new chapter in their lives.

XVIII

RECKONING ON THE MOUNTAIN OF ENLIGHTENMENT

The short plane trip culminated in an unforgettable descent into the Kathmandu Valley. They had heard reports of a treacherous approach and landing into the airport, however the experience of it proved to be nothing other than totally exhilarating.

After being processed through immigration, they collected their luggage and exited the doors that cordoned off incoming visitors from the hectic scene of the world outside. They looked out, beyond the crowd of taxi drivers and people milling about, in search of Swami. They had met him once before, back at the sound healing centre, so were familiar with his tranquil face and peaceful demeanour. Noah caught glimpse of a hand waving, but it wasn't Swami.

Instead, a Tibetan monk had caught his attention, and appeared to be perhaps waiting to greet a group of visitors eager to learn the art of meditation. Noah smiled warmly at the monk who immediately smiled back, his eyes alight and his heart bursting with the flames of love. Noah could see his energy projecting out, as a faint luminous haze just around the perimeter of his body. It was not the first time Noah had perceived of auric fields. Since the *Flu*, he had experienced an elevation in his abilities, feeling energy more acutely, and now also visually seeing the life force, the aura, surrounding plants, birds, people and other living things.

'There's Swami,' Aurora exclaimed. She nudged Noah, who seemed to have drifted off into a daze.

'Oh! Great!' Noah said, still somewhat distracted by the exchange with the monk.

'Did you see that monk standing there?' Noah asked of Aurora.

'No? Where?' Aurora looked over in the direction he had been staring. Noah scanned the area, but to his surprise, the monk was gone.

The journey from the airport to the hotel was rather uneventful. Swami's delight at the pairs arrival was obvious, expressing excitement for the couple to learn the craft of the bowls.

'Here we are. This is your accommodation. I will see you in the morning for our first lesson however, till then, should you need anything, please just come next door and ask for me. I'm always available between time in meditation and tutelage of the bowls,' Swami bidding the couple a good evening.

The porter escorted them to their room. It was the room that had been promised by Otto, the one with a view of the iconic temple. Excitedly, Noah drew the curtains back and flung open the timber shutters; in flowed the exotic smells, as too did the hustle and bustle of the street below. In the near distance, some hundred metres away, stood the grandiose Boudhanath Stupa, over-powering the small guesthouse as it rose upward toward the heavens. The colourful prayer flags swayed in the afternoon breeze, and the compassionate eyes of Buddha gazed out over the valley. Given it hadn't been a long flight and both had managed to sleep on the plane, a quick shower and refresh was all they needed before venturing out into the labyrinth.

Swami had given directions to a nearby restaurant, recommending a local dish, *Thukpa,* as appropriate nourishment to offset any adverse effects of the flight. Noah and Aurora were quite chuffed in learning that *Thukpa,* was a traditional Himalayan noodle soup, sharing similarities with their cherished chicken broth. They had chuckled at the irony of the suggestion, for it was a novel idea to sit and drink of the salubrious elixir, such a distance away from their kitchen. Much the same as theirs, the secret to soulful nourishing *Thukpa* was the stock, however, the Nepalese version generally featured spicier flavours. From the basis of the stock, the dish is customised, from a variety of choices, according to taste, by adding either mushrooms, dried fish, lamb, lean chicken or yak meat. The soup is celebrated to be a complete meal in itself, with just three rudimentary components — carbohydrates from noodles, fibre from vegetables and protein from meat. Furthermore, the couple were also charmed to discover that its name denoted it as being a 'heart warming dish,' for in Tibet, the word *'thuk'* literally translates to heart.

A short ten minute walk across the square, through busy cobbled streets, full of stalls, artisans, people and motorbikes, brought them to the modest little eatery they were searching for. They ordered the soup, selecting it be served with dried fish, and requested the chef go easy on the heat. Taking recommendation from the waiter, they also decided on another traditional dish, *Aloo Kauli,* prepared with potato, cauliflower and spices, which in the opinion of the man was unmissable. The vegetable dish was interesting and they enjoyed its unique depth of flavour. The soup brimmed with all the goodness it was accustomed for, and the fish, whilst not being so much to Aurora's liking, provided a good source of protein and healthy fats.

After relishing the culinary delights, the couple slowly made their way through the maze of alleyways and longer strips, pausing to look into the windows of many stores displaying the most fascinating of crystals, naturally occurring in the region. There was a buzz in the air, musicians played the *Madal* and children danced in the streets, awash in the fragrant scent of incense that permeated. Reaching the guesthouse and their room, they journaled in the sitting area, snuffed out the candles, shut the windows and turned in for the night. It had now passed eleven and the need for a restful sleep resigned Noah's desire for intimacy take a back seat.

The town woke, the streets came alive and the couple made way downstairs for breakfast before going next door for their first lesson with Swami. The program for that day encompassed learning the history of the singing bowls, how they were fashioned and how each served its own purpose tuned to a specific frequency. Before concluding, Swami instructed the couple to lay down, so that he could take them through a series of chakra cleansings. As he proceeded to play through the sequence of the bowls, the room was imbued with each distinctive vibration. The healing energy transmitted made one feel still, quiet and unified — it was immensely peaceful. Once again, Noah had been visited by the coppery light. It was a reminder of Gabriel's presence, and of the guidance that had stood since the first encounter. The tears of that last meeting had ceased, the bearing down in the heart space had vanished and Noah breathed with the confidence of a person now floodlit by the light. This confirmation, the energy of the angel so apparent, served as yet another synchronistic example that he had remained in the flow of the heart space.

It was late morning by the time the couple had finished their three hours of tuition. Prior to leaving for the trip, Noah had made a shortlist of the best cafes in town. He had a passionate appreciation for coffee, and knew the region as being renowned for its high altitude mountain grown organic varieties. The Himalayas were particularly fertile; the soils and climate ideally suited to the cultivation of thriving crops of arabica. Over their travels he had favoured that which originated from Sumatra, but was eager to compare, and taste the coffee on another continent, with different growing conditions.

'Let's go to a cafe and talk over espresso, I'd really love one now.' Noah said.

'Yes, sure,' Aurora swiftly replied.

Noah was duly impressed by Aurora's interest in something she wasn't all that interested in. With some gusto and a spring in his step, he took her hand and made way for the cafe.

'Let's walk down this lane, I believe towards the end is where the best coffee shop in town is. They run an Italian machine with an award-winning barista, and it rates highly on all the normally critical traveller reviews.'

Along the way, the colourful happenings of the town left an indelible mark on them — it was a place of vibrance, diversity and rich spiritual history. The buildings, some old, some restored and some new, portrayed the unmistakable quaintness of the place. Hikers passed by, frantically marching onwards on whatever adventure they were on. Climbers stopped and peered into the windows of stores, offering all manner of gear for the intrepid and courageous. It was a fast paced scene of remarkable wonder, yet tranquil at the same time.

'Here it is,' Noah exclaimed, delighted to have found the cafe. 'Oh the smell! Can you smell the beans?'

'Yes, it smells wonderful,' Aurora agreed, frolicking in the majesty of the place that she had only before imagined. Everything carried a distinct and prominent smell, everything a characteristic flavour, a special texture and an individuated energy. This was a place of curiosity, unlike anywhere they'd ever been before, yet there was an unexplainable familiarity to it.

'Aah, that's great,' Noah having savoured the first sip of the expertly crafted cappuccino, brewed with locally sourced beans from the slopes of the mid-hills.

'This coffee has such a creamy body with a woody aroma, I can taste the subtle notes of cranberry, prunes and orange. It's quite beautiful coffee really.'

He was savoring the long-awaited experience, which richly delivered on his expectations. Noah momentarily placed down his cappuccino on the small rustic table made from reclaimed wood.

'I've been meaning to talk to you and share what I experienced back there at the airport,' Noah began.

He outlined that when he'd walked through the doors to the outside, he had expected it to feel foreign and unfamiliar, yet immediately sensed an unexplainable familiarity.

'I had an urge to speak the words, *I'm home,* without any real inclination as to why I would want to say that...I thought it was perhaps due to the Tibetan influence here.'

Noah returning to his coffee having found difficulty in detailing exactly what he had felt.

'Go on, continue. I'm interested to hear more,' Aurora lovingly encouraged him to elaborate.

'Well, I caught glimpse of a monk. First I saw his hand, from out of nowhere, it stood out amongst all the baggage, the people, the drivers and tour operators in wait. I traced his hand down toward his face. It was weathered, yet youthful, stern yet solemn, he shone brightly amongst the others. I could see his aura, feel his heart.'

Noah expressed that he had felt a connection beyond that of the physical, it was a higher sensory connection, one of recognition and relevance.

'Then I felt a conscious transition of sorts, as if I had been thrust into a portal, a glitch in the matrix of third dimensional reality,' he continued.

'It was a deep feeling of remembrance. I saw myself here before, when no airport stood on this land. I saw myself draped in orange walking alongside the monk, carrying the wisdom and the contentment of the truth. I saw myself as a disciple of the dimensions, as the highest embodiment of my spirit in living form. I was whole.'

He continued to describe how he had lost track of time, and how it appeared to have stood still. He felt as though he had experienced space in time, as opposed to the regular experience of time in space. It was a moment of zero point, that was of the now, but also of the past and of the future simultaneously. His perception of reality had been neither of this world, or another, it had been of pure space, and a distinctly recognisable integration with the everything. The couple debated the disparity between the amount of time that had actually elapsed in Noah's fleeting exchange with the monk; Noah had perceived it as being far longer than Aurora had.

Having finished his coffee, thanking the barista for the experience, Noah suggested they move onward in their explorations. Since undertaking the research on Nepal back home in the tropics, he'd always planned to surprise Aurora by taking her to visit a special place that he knew she'd appreciate. Till now, he'd kept it a secret, waiting for the perfect moment on the trip to arise. With the sun shining so brightly high up in the sky, he saw this as the ideal time.

They headed in the direction of the idyllic Garden of Dreams. Along the way, Noah serendipitously spotted a large bazaar, spontaneously giving him an idea to further surprise Aurora with a picnic. Whilst Aurora scouted the abundance of intricate textiles, artwork, clothing and collectible items, Noah made his way over towards the food vendors. He browsed the numerous little stalls of enticing cute cut sandwiches, and the array of pre-packed lunches for hikers, selecting an appetizing spread based on his love's likes and dislikes.

Soon after, they arrived at what is often referred to as the Garden of the Gods, and it was just that — a prolific garden of heavenly respite. Neo-classical in its design, it featured three pavilions, an amphitheater, ponds, pergolas and an abundance of flora, manicured hedges and fountains. They sat on the fine grass and laid out the hamper of sweet and savoury treats, eating lunch in the secluded spot, near a small fish pond dignified with lotus flowers. Aurora was ever so grateful for Noah's thoughtfulness, as she loved the wholesome novelty of a traditional picnic in botanical gardens. They stared out over the tranquil waters listening to the chirping of the birds and the temple bells ringing out over the cityscape. It was an ideal spot, quiet and sheltered from the chaotic traffic outside, and possessed an enchanting presence. It reminded Noah somewhat of the mystical and surreal type of energy he'd felt when they'd visited Tirta Empul, a Balinese water temple.

Two days had passed, and they had successfully graduated from the intensive course in sound therapy. Both were enjoying the town for all its traditional food, inexpensive handmade items, unique trinkets and sites of historical importance. It was everything and more than they had fathomed. In line with their edict of going with the flow, they made various enquiries into taking a day trip into the mountains, not to Everest or to base camp, but into the foothills where a Tibetan monastery had been established centuries ago.

Swami offered to escort them, for which the couple gratefully accepted; they had heard of the undulating roads and steep drops, so preferred the assurance of Swami's Jeep, rather than a shonky tour bus. Noah dressed in quintessentially hippie garb — yoga pants, a linen shirt and sandals he had bought from a local shoemaker. He had taken a liking to the shoemaker who was a ripe ninety-two years young, still masterfully creating treads for earth conscious travellers to adorn on their ways, like the pilgrims of old.

The monastery was a particular place of interest for Noah, he had read much about the *Gompa*, the monks and the meditation classes held there. He was drawn to the monastery as being a spiritual haven, where one could withdraw from the temporal world, and seek renunciation from one's materialistic and sensual desires. It was a place teaching the central philosophies of right attitude and right action, with which the couple both aligned. They were driven by a desire to learn the ancient ways of dissolving all sense of separation, thereby deepening their connection with God.

The drive up the mountain was breathtaking. In the distance the magnificence of the Himalayan peaks were clear to see, the blue sky meeting its earthly giants and the sun bathing them in golden light. Curious little dwellings, stony roads, wise old women, colourful flags and signposts directing climbers to where they were headed, all made for a stimulating collage. It was memorable, the air crisp, pure and cleansing. Swami spoke of the history and of the momentous naturally occurring events that had apparently carved this place into its grandeur and eternal significance.

Reaching the monastery, the couple touched foreheads, exchanged a soft kiss and with some stiffness exited the car that had been their chariot into this uncharted realm. Two monks greeted the pair at the entrance, adjacent to the main *Gompa*. With characteristically warm smiles both Noah and Aurora greeted them with a bow of respect, for which the monks duly reciprocated.

'Namaste,' the monk cheerfully honoured the divine in the pair.

'This is a place of peace,' he continued.

'A place where one can achieve complete stillness and deeply feel into the connection to the all. We trust you will find your time here fulfilling, empowering and transformational.'

Perhaps he had repeated the same greeting a thousand times before, but he delivered it with the sincerity of the first.

'The group meditation will commence shortly. Would you like to join today? Otherwise, given you've just arrived, you may prefer to dedicate your own time in private meditation in the garden. We have many beautiful, tranquil areas to sit and contemplate.'

Noah and Aurora considered the alternative, deeming it would be best to take their time. The ascent up the mountain had taken longer than expected, and they couldn't help but to feel a little rushed.

'I'm sure you'll find a spot that resonates somewhere on the grounds,' said the monk.

He pointed over toward the path that led to the garden proper and smiled to the couple as they made their way to the opening, framed by a little wrought iron gate.

The garden opened out into an expanse of soft deep green lawns, precisely manicured shrubs and delicate beds of flowers bursting with lustrous colour. There were magnificent trees throughout, each offering a small bench beside them for one to sit and rest. Every forty meters or so, paved in natural stone, were small circular areas inlaid into the lawn. As Noah and Aurora progressed further into the fascinating landscape, they noticed a monk carefully planting marigolds. Having sensed their approach he stopped, turned and smiled radiantly at them. Noah gently prodded Aurora.

'That's the same monk that I saw at the airport, I'm certain of it.'

Noah was particularly thrilled with this unexpected, yet synchronous sighting of what he adamantly concluded to be the same very monk. The monk appeared to have completed his duties, as all the pots that had contained the plants were empty. They decided to walk over and introduce themselves. Moreover, the couple wanted to express their appreciation for the flowers he had planted, and show gratitude for the garden which was one of the most beautiful they'd ever seen.

Observant of Noah and Aurora's curiosity and apparent gratitude, the monk explained the significance of the marigold in Buddhist philosophy.

'The warm nature of the flower, as exemplified by its fiery yellow, orange and red hues, strongly ties it to the sun. These colours signify renunciation and are the colours we use during our rituals in various ways, to signify surrender to the higher being.'

He noted that marigolds are known to have protective properties, and further symbolised trust and faith in the divine, imbuing one with a will to overcome obstacles.

The monk, who had obviously warmed to the couple's kindliness, then conveyed a wish for them to accompany him on a guided walk through the gardens. As he softly paced along the path, the couple were enthralled by his detailed explanation of the history of the monastery. The monk stopped in front of a pond of lilies, and leant over to glance into the water below. He contemplated a moment, before standing back up and proposing that they both join him for time in meditation. Noah and Aurora gladly accepted the impromptu invitation.

'Thank you,' they both responded in recognition of the rare opportunity to sit with the wise.

The monk then motioned to move onward in the direction of a grand tree that stood majestically over the others; this was where they would find his personal space of solitude. As he slowly chaperoned the couple down the winding pathway, the monk stopped intermittently to smell certain flowers, and detail the reasons for their inclusion in the garden. He appeared to enjoy being in the company of the two, and was particularly impressed with their genuine interest in the array of flora that he proudly tended to. He made comment in acknowledgement of this, pausing in front of a sweeping line of indigo flowers.

'I can sense a high frequency around you both. It is clear to me that you exemplify the few, those who have applied themselves to the work of the spirit.'

As they continued on further, he directed them off the main route and toward the right. As soon as they turned the corner, Noah and Aurora caught a glimpse of the serene spot he was leading them to. The view out into the mountains was unlike any the couple had ever seen; seven peaks, all over seven thousand meters tall, reached up into the heavens. As they drew closer with each step, the captivating area revealed itself. It was a gently terraced, grassy expanse at the very edge of the property. In the centre, stood a spectacular old tree with an intricately twisted trunk. The couple instantly knew it to be a place where divine energies emanated from the Earth. The monk turned his head toward the couple, fixing his eyes on Noah, and proudly illustrated that this sacred tree marked the arrival at their destination. He then proceeded in melodious monologue, guided by forces greater than his mortal self -

'Dearest one, I feel you have toiled in striving to attain that which you have long sought. You have struggled through futility, and a fragility that impacted how you lived your life. Your being was muddy and confused, its desolate perception saw you fearful over the future. You have carried pain, guilt, mistrust and disillusionment with the world, upon your shoulders. You have stood in the face of death, as a victim to the emotional bacteria of your past and the infection of your mind.

There has been many like you, many who do not experience what it is to be living. Some are choosing to depart this realm, whilst others fall at the hand of self-inflicted fate. Some are submitting to their own sabotage and others succumbing to calamity. Many are blind, unable to sustain themselves in their own light, living automatically and unconsciously, afraid of a future that they themselves have the power to manifest. For you have all suffered a contagious virus of consciousness, confined to a limited scope of possibility.

But you, dear one, you have experienced the dissolution of your mortal fears, and have overcome the separation, the fear of abandonment and a lonely state of isolation. You have passed the test of your spiritual decay and awakened into a heightened state of awareness. You have risen into the higher heart and expanded your reality into the wondrous sensory luminosity of the third eye.

Angelic beings have decontaminated your ego, cleansed you of your subconscious debris and supported you through the fight against the demons of darkness. Your guides have mirrored your breath, through your journey in discovering the peace you now pervade this day. This marks your timely awakening and your resurrection following a period of purification. You have awakened into the truth of who you really are, the spiritual being you truly are.

Your soul is illuminated once again, and your earthly spirit has been re-ignited. The light is of you, it follows you, it guides you and it enlightens all aspects of you. Follow the corridors of consciousness, the passage to your enlightenment, the state at which you are the promise of everything, and all you have the potential to be. Follow this passage, always. From the spiralling underside of the flower to the awareness of the hawk carrying himself upon the warm winds of the aethers, through numbers presented to you and visionary experiences over your lifetime, walk forward in the knowing that you are innerconnected with all.'

The monk stopped there and deeply inhaled, cleansing himself of the long divination. In this moment, Noah strongly perceived that an awakening had been gifted to him, however, he wasn't clear as to when that moment of awakening had taken place. Was it the moment when his soul was purged of the virus, and his body detoxified of the *Flu*? Or was it the moment when he realised the potential for him to grant his love the gift of a child? Could it have been when he reached the ultimate reconciliation of the emotional and psychological ghosts of his past? Or was it a transcendent combination of all these happenings in their synchronous individuality; a divinely orchestrated synthesis of his soul history, his life experience, his learnings and his dedicated commitment to self-mastery? It didn't matter.

'Thank you...' Noah whispered with overwhelm.

'Your words are so profound to us and we appreciate your wisdom.'

Noah's curiosity at the immensity of what the monk had said, placed him in a state where he could hardly repress his own astonishment. Aurora had equally been moved beyond words with the vastness of the concepts that the monk had detailed, and tears begun to flow down her face. She had longed to see Noah happy, with real purpose, his purpose. She knew the significance of the trip for him. He was on his personal journey through which the passage to his destiny was laid out before him. He was on the precipice of great things, of becoming his potential and never relapsing into the Noah of old.

'Let us meditate,' the monk said, directing the couple to sit on the grass in the cool shade of the tree.

With the great mountains as witness, it was time to go within. The monk took his place only inches away from Noah. The three adopted the Sukhasana posture, in complete silence, with the monk instructing the couple to commence the deep breathing required to achieve the meditative state. Noah could feel the aura winging out from the man, and felt a rare peace in his presence. Within minutes they were immersed in a deep state of relaxation, their breath naturally harmonising into the flow of one.

Noah was thrust into infinite space, propelled beyond the stars, upwards through the dimensions, the densities and out into the cosmos, the realm of truth. It was black, then light, then filled with splendiferous colours opening up into an expanse that was equally everything and anything that ever was, is or could ever be. He sat above the Earth, from a higher realm of perception, where the observer is the creator and the creator is the observer. He witnessed the world as though it was on an axis, for which he could at his whim, turn, stop and project his vision inwards into the essence, the spirit, the time, the scene of any place he chose to explore.

He peered into a vast land, the country or continent wasn't of any relevance. He was not observing of the world as he had before, there were no borders, except for those created by Earth itself, by the lands meeting the oceans. He viewed a world rejuvenated, reborn in the frequency of love, living in harmony as one being, one community and one spirit. He saw that the global collective had broken the shackles, transcending the malignance of the *Spiritual Flu*. The Earth had transfigured and the people that had transgressed so greatly, had passed, transiting onward in their journey, leaving behind a revitalised planet and ascended people living an expansive experience. The people were kind and respected the environment. They lived as one with Mother Earth. The towns and its inhabitants had once again moved back into, and in tune with nature. The Earth had undergone its own reckoning, the times of the decay had passed and the gestation of the new world had run its course. It was a world that had finally achieved the dimensional shift and transited into the space of love and unity. It had been returned to an age of enlightenment once again.

Noah's vision was drawn to a part of the world that he had never seen before, perhaps this was an alternate world, in an alternate reality, he grappled. It was an island set deep in the heart of the vast sea that wrapped the planet. He projected his awareness further to discover the most transcending truth of all; he was able to see himself and Aurora, playing joyfully with a child, *their* child. His daughter, a small girl with golden chestnut locks that curled down to her shoulders, blazing blue eyes like the waters of Polynesia, skin of pure olive and a smile that splashed a ten meter radius with a blinding indigo light. It was a psychedelic, kaleidoscopic and transcendent moment.

Noah then felt some movement, and sensed the slight alteration in Aurora's breath, alerting him that she returned from meditation. He had witnessed what he had been destined to. He had witnessed a new world upon which a new him resided, with Aurora, and their precious child, amongst a unified community of people. People that had held the critical mass long enough for the world to ascend, and to never relive its misguided past. They were in permanent remission; the most radical shift possible had overcome all.

Noah opened his eyes, coming back into the full conscious awareness of the surrounds.

Aurora looked astonished.

'Where's the monk?' she asked.

'What do you mean?' Noah added, completely baffled.

Noah looked around, the monk was nowhere to be seen, he had literally disappeared without a trace. Increasingly bemused by this, the couple nonchalantly ventured back toward the main entrance where Swami was soon to meet them. As they walked, they looked left and right, checking each of the many small secluded sections on either side of the path, but there was no sign of the monk.

They reached the entrance and were greeted by the same two monks with which they had originally conversed upon arrival. One of the monks enquired as to how they had enjoyed their time in the gardens, to which both Noah and Aurora conveyed their sincere appreciation. Noah couldn't help but to make enquiries about the monk who had been gardening, the one they had bonded with. Given he had all but vanished, the couple hadn't an opportunity to personally thank him for the experience they'd shared, considering it had delivered such profound insight. He inquisitively asked the monks if they knew where he was, to which they replied, that no monks were assigned to gardening duties that day.

'All the monks have been occupied today in the main *Gompa*, giving blessing to the large group.'

The monk clearly confirmed that all monks residing on the property had been accounted for. The couple were tremendously perplexed, adding that the monk they were referencing, had been at the airport earlier that week. The two monks adamantly informed Noah that the priory seldom visited town, and unless they were embarking on a pilgrimage, they had no reason at all to travel — their life of dedication and solitude largely confined them to the monastery. Neither of the men were able to offer any explanation and appeared as equally bewildered as the couple.

Noah and Aurora bid the friendly monks farewell, thanking them again. As they walked over to where Swami had been patiently waiting, Noah turned to Aurora.

'I'm absolutely positive that was the same monk I exchanged with at the airport. He looked exactly the same, same facial features, skin tone, demeanour and stature. It had to be!'

Given Noah's prior experience, Aurora questioned whether or not the monk had indeed even been present back at the airport. Whether perhaps he was not of this world, as though it was now more likely they had been touched by an angel, a guide or even a messenger of God, perhaps Gabriel himself. They both came to the conclusion that whatever had manifested in the form of the monk, was prolific in its wisdom, and a messenger of divine origins.

Upon their return back down the hillsides, through the small villages and back into town, the couple shared a soothing hot shower. Noah lathered Aurora's hair and gently rinsed it off, avoiding getting any soap in her eyes. Aurora feeling rejuvenated, changed into a clean set of clothes. Noah lagging behind, stood under the flow of the hot water as it rained down onto his shaven head, cleansing his crown chakra. Having just finished in the ensuite's waterfall, Noah saw his phone flashing and vibrating over on the dresser.

'Hey honey,' Noah yelled out, with a towel wrapped around him. He was dripping wet and didn't want to slip on the floor running to answer it.

'Can you answer the phone, I'm saturated…I'm not sure who would be calling us at this time, but best you check.'

'Oh! Sorry, okay, I'll answer it,' the voice from the other side of the room bellowed out. Aurora had her head out the window observing the goings on down in the alley below; she was fixated on a lady that had set up a stall full of gleaming crystals.

'Hello, this is Aurora speaking.'

'Hi dear, may I speak with Noah please?'

Aurora didn't recognise the voice on the other end of the line; it was a sophisticated mature-aged woman, who spoke with eloquence.

'Yes. Sure, I'll just get him for you. Please hold for a moment.'

'Who is it?' Noah enquired.

'It's an officious sounding woman, who has asked to speak to you. I didn't ask her name, anyhow, you better see what she wants.'

Noah took the phone.

'Hi, this is Noah.'

'Hello Noah, pleased to finally speak with you. I have been following you since you self-published your first work, your book some months ago. I wanted to praise you for your courage, and for your success in writing such a wonderful story,' the woman paused.

'Oh...' Noah responded, momentarily lost for words.

'Thank you very much. That means a lot to me. I have put my heart and my soul into that work and feel the most fulfilled I ever have in my life,' Noah gleefully returning the woman's heartfelt sentiment.

'I must formally introduce myself,' the woman continued.

'My name is Betty and I am calling on behalf of the Chairman. I represent one of the world's leading publishing houses for titles spiritual in nature. We contact you with a proposition in mind, and would like to offer you a long-term publishing contract.'

Noah was now speechless, and looked over to Aurora, who was listening to the conversation on loudspeaker.

The company was most impressed with preliminary sales and the multitude of positive reader reviews. The woman outlined that their mindful management would assure that Noah's message would reach further into the global market. She conveyed that they were specifically motivated in ensuring that his inspirational story of perseverance, awakening and of ascension into a richer experience of one's life, would receive the exposure it was worthy of.

'We loved your novel and feel it only prudent to take you under our wing. We are committed to see to it, that your work of great revelation and encouragement, contributes to changing lives, by offering those on the path, an uplifting story of liberation to relate to. Many people globally are searching for hope, for context and are desperate for a glimpse of the light. They are the ones, within the many, who are striving to find inner peace, searching for a better way of being and praying for a new world to dawn. We are the wings upon which your inspiring message will be spread far and wide across the world, and once this book has been enjoyed by millions, then so too, will your next,' said Betty.

'Have you written again after writing this tale Noah?'

'Yes! And I have a great title for it too. I'll keep you in suspense for now, but what I will tell you is that, it's an epic love story.'

Tears flowed down Noah's eyes, this was the moment of transcendence, his moment of becoming.

He became the earth, the wind, the sky, the sun, the stars, the universe. He had returned to the place from which he had originated, eternity.

He was now the embodiment of the very light he had since birth, searched to rediscover. He was now one, creating the life he lived.

ABOUT THE AUTHOR

Justin Stewart is an Australian born international healer,
visionary writer and metaphysical philosopher.

Through his literary work, he masterfully courses the
imaginations of readers, chartering them through mystical
journeys that awaken the mind and illuminate the soul.

His vivid exploration of the magical, and navigation
through the emerging realm of spiritual science,
propels us into a world of wonder and infinite possibility.

✳

To learn more about Justin and his work
in service to humanity, please visit his website.

justinstewart.au

ALSO BY THIS AUTHOR

the
twin
flames

FROM THE AUTHOR OF 'THE SPIRITUAL FLU'
JUSTIN STEWART

AN EPIC TALE OF DIVINE LOVE